Get back there and put ⸻ soldier barks. She moves toward us with the ID scanner.

"But —"

"LINE UP AND SHUT UP!" she shouts. "Get your bracelets where I can see them."

This is it. The end. Through her teeth Rosie whispers, "Take the others and go. I'll create a —"

I see a flash of yellow out of the corner of my eye like a scarf. I hear a *whoooooooooosh* and the area fills with smoke.

I can't see a thing but someone grabs my hand and Rosie's voice in my ear says "Run" and I do.

We run together, tripping, directly into the cloud of acrid smoke. My lungs are burning and my eyes are stinging and I can barely keep them open.

When the smoke begins to thin, I see that Louisa is holding Rosie's other hand. But Alonso, Drew, and Ryan have vanished.

TOMORROW GIRLS

Behind the Gates

Run for Cover

With the Enemy

Set Me Free

TOMORROW GIRLS

With the Enemy

BY EVA GRAY

SCHOLASTIC INC.

New York   Toronto   London   Auckland
Sydney   Mexico City   New Delhi   Hong Kong

No part of this publication may be reproduced, stored in a retrieval system, or transmitted in any form or by any means, electronic, mechanical, photocopying, recording, or otherwise, without written permission of the publisher. For information regarding permission, write to: Scholastic Inc., Attention: Permissions Department, 557 Broadway, New York, NY 10012.

ISBN 978-0-545-31703-0

Copyright © 2011 by Michele Jaffe.
All rights reserved. Published by Scholastic Inc.
SCHOLASTIC and associated logos are trademarks and/or registered trademarks of Scholastic Inc.

12 11 10 9 8 7 6 5 4 3   12 13 14 15 16/0

Printed in the U.S.A.   40
First printing, September 2011

Sometimes if you can't think of an answer, it's because the answer is unthinkable.

Chapter 1

My vision is blurry. I don't know if it's from tears or from the shimmering of the diesel fuel hovering over the hot pavement.

She's gone. I can't believe Maddie is gone.

I have spent a lot of my life playing "What's the worst that could happen?" in my head. Given that I am growing up in the middle of a war, I have some pretty good scenarios — total annihilation and starvation, obviously. But there's SO MUCH stuff before that (think snakes and spiders just to start with). Mostly, none of it ever came true.

Until now.

Five minutes ago, I thought finding out that my fancy boarding school was controlled by a ruthless enemy organization called the Alliance, and then being on the run from them with no food, no identity bracelet, and no money, was The Worst Thing that Could Happen Ever.

But then the masked assailants with the eyes of stone-cold killers drove an unmarked black truck into the parking lot of the mall my friends and I had been hiding in. They plucked one of my friends up like a bird of prey grabbing a helpless field mouse and roared off with her, totally raising The Worst bar.

Which is a lesson: never start thinking of The Worst because there is always something Worse out there.

The moment of Maddie Frye's kidnapping will be imprinted on every one of my senses forever. The scent of diesel exhaust hanging in the warm air. The knee-melting rumble of the engine ringing in my ears. The dry-mouthed horror of watching Drew throw his body in front of the speeding vehicle in a vain effort to stop it. The feel of my braids whipping against my cheek as my head spun around to follow the zigzag path of the truck.

The wild, terrified expression in Louisa's big blue eyes and the hysterical tone in her voice as she turns to me now and says, "We have to find her." She grabs the edges of my red down vest with the heart-shaped quilting my mother insisted on. "We have to figure out where she is. Evelyn, where is she?"

Louisa Ballinger is Maddie's first, official best friend from home. The two of them were best friends for years before we were all sent to Country Manor School; in fact, they pretended to be sisters so that Maddie would be accepted, since CMS was only for the children of the rich and elite. (I pointed out to my parents that this smacked of evil intentions but they did that thing where they simultaneously roll their eyes and ignore me.)

In the past Louisa hasn't always been the biggest fan of my Ask Now, Be Prepared Later philosophy, so it is kind of surprising that she's turning to me at this moment. But I'm glad.

"I don't kno —" I begin.

"You always know," she interrupts, shaking me with all her athlete's strength. "You are always thinking of things. Think of something. Think. You have to. *Please.*"

"I will," I say. "I promise."

3

I have capital *N* capital *O* business saying anything like that. I only say it because it seems like the right thing to do. And I guess it is, because Louisa stops looking quite so panicked. When Ryan comes over to her, she even manages a tiny smile.

Now what?

I glance at Rosie Chavez for guidance. Up to now she's been our unofficial leader and has done an amazing job. But the brown eyes that meet mine, usually fierce and alive, are empty. Like she is not really there. Even the gold band holding her dark ponytail seems to have lost its glint.

I guess she is blaming herself for what happened to Maddie. Rosie was sleeping at the time, but only because she'd been working so hard to make sure we all survived. Without her, Maddie, Louisa, and I never would have made it away from the girls' section of CMS. Even when we were joined by Drew, Alonso, and Ryan, who'd escaped from the boys' section (which meant three more people to hide, not to mention feed, and boys eat a lot), she managed to keep us going. We got through the woods, out of an Alliance prison camp, and to where we are now, which by my calculations is about twenty-five miles from our homes in Chicago.

"This isn't your fault," I say to Rosie.

She stares not at me but through me, not fluttering an eyelid. I'm not sure she can even hear.

Drew, our second-best leader, is standing with his forehead resting against the siding of the mall. His arms are crossed over his chest, his eyes are pressed shut behind his silver-framed glasses, and his jaw is tight. Alonso, hand over his mouth and dark hair falling over his eyes, looks like a statue called Boy in Shock.

This isn't good. Someone needs to do something. And I realize that maybe this time the someone is me.

"We should go back inside, at least for now," I say, struggling to sound how I think Rosie would sound. "Regroup." My official tone and the leader-y lingo feel a little foreign to me. While it's true that I talk a lot, usually people just laugh or sigh or say, "Does anyone beside Miss Posner have a question?" or "Evelyn, darling, please not tonight; your mother has a headache." I'm not used to people actually *listening*.

But, astonishingly, they do. And even stranger is the way Alonso approaches me and, pushing his hair out of his eyes, says, "Is it okay if I take a second out here?" As though I'm actually in charge.

"Um, sure," I tell him, and follow the others as they drift back toward the abandoned mall.

I notice that Ryan's blue eyes keep darting to Louisa, to make sure she's okay, and I'm grateful to him. Drew keeps his head bowed, his posture mirroring Rosie's stooped shoulders as he walks next to her.

When we first got to the mall, I remember taking in its soaring ceiling, wide-open space, and the tracery of vines clinging to the walls. I thought it was almost mystical, like an abandoned pagan temple.

Now it feels like a dusty crypt.

We scale the silent escalators to the second floor and head past the Tie Palace and Apollo Tans, back to the corner where we'd been sitting before Maddie was taken.

Rosie leans against one of the planters that still holds dried-out vines from when the mall was one of the Shopping Wonders of the World (according to the promotional poster I saw on the floor of the Dido Wedding Salon). Ryan perches on a bench next to Louisa, his red hair almost brown with matted dust. Drew sits next to the wall, his face unreadable. I've never seen him so . . . disengaged. I wonder if it's because he'd been out searching for food with Maddie right before she was taken, and now he's feeling guilty, too.

Great.

As my gaze shifts I realize everyone is looking at me expectantly.

My knees feel like they're made of Jell-O, and I sink more than sit down on the floor. For possibly the first time in my life, my mind is completely blank. It is like it has been bleached clean by shock. The idea that Maddie is gone is both impossible and agonizing. Because even though Maddie and I had only known each other a short time, she had been my best friend at CMS. Maybe my best friend ever.

My parents hold hands under the breakfast table. They think I don't notice, but I do. I'm not sure they're even totally aware of it; it's like they love each other so much they can't help touching each other.

They love me, too, of course, and they are great parents. But sometimes the intensity of their feelings for each other makes me feel like an outsider.

That's why, even though I suspected CMS was a little sinister, I was excited to go to boarding school. I was looking forward to making friends and being part of a group. Having people want to have breakfast with *me*. Being included.

As bad as CMS was — not the facilities, which were very nice, but the unfortunate part about it being a covert enemy-training facility — I felt like I belonged. And the best part was Maddie.

Is Maddie, I correct myself. She's going to be fine. We're going to find her and rescue her.

I pull a rubber band out of my backpack and wrestle my braids into a ponytail. I force my brain to work. Okay. Maddie has been taken. We don't know by whom. We don't know where. This is hopeless. We know nothing.

Nothing.

"That's it," I say aloud. "Nothing."

Everyone looks at me like they wish they had

something handy to throw at my head (and Alonso probably would have, too, but he's not back yet).

I explain myself quickly. "There were no markings on the car that took Maddie, right? Nothing written on it?"

Ryan sits forward, his blue eyes beginning to sparkle with interest. Louisa's head tilts to one side. Rosie glances up from the inspection she's been making of the ends of her hair. Drew frowns like he is running a play-by-play through his mind. He'd been the closest to the vehicle. He says, "None visible."

I nod. "Exactly. And since the economy fizzled, how many official vehicles have you seen without *something* written on them?"

Ryan gives a low whistle. "You're right. In my neighborhood, the police are sponsored by Peaceful Night sleeping pills and the siren sounds kind of like a lullaby."

"You're lucky," Drew says. His voice sounds oddly strained, tight. "Near my old house they drive around in cars that are painted to look like bathroom tile with the Plumber's Pal slogan, 'We send scum down the drain,' and the siren makes a toilet-flushing noise. I heard

Wrinkle Away made a bid to sponsor the presidential limo."

"No way," I say. "I never even read that rumor. Is that why the president decided —"

Louisa breaks in then, speaking in this strange, faraway voice, her gaze unfixed. "The last army tank I saw was sponsored by Seedie's Sweets. I couldn't figure out why they would sponsor a tank, but then Maddie said maybe because they were *dangerously* delicious and —" She stops in midsentence. Her gaze focuses on us now and it is full of pain. "You guys didn't know but she — she could be really funny like that. Oh no." Tears fill her eyes and instinctively I put my arm around her. The boys act like there's suddenly something really interesting to look at in the other direction.

"All right," I go on. "So the truck that took Maddie had no logos on it. Either it belonged to some private company or some supersecret government organization —"

"Or an organization that isn't supposed to be here. Like the Alliance," Rosie finishes for me. The way she is looking at me is new. Instead of "Oh, seriously, please," her expression seems to say, "Nice work. Tell me more."

Color starts to flood back into Louisa's face and she wipes her eyes. "Wait. If it's the Alliance, that means they are probably taking her back to that prison we saw." She plants her feet and starts to stand. "The one near the border. We should go."

I really don't want to have to be the one to remind her it has taken us a day and a half riding in the back of a truck to get from there to here. Not to mention we don't even know where the prison is.

"It might," I say, stalling, "but —"

"Chicago," a voice pants from below us. We all rush to the edge of the balcony.

Alonso is standing on the ground floor, bent over with his hands on his knees. He looks up and smiles this kind of mischievous smile he has. Not that I've really noticed.

"The transport that took Maddie? It headed in the direction of Chicago. I found fresh tire marks on the road."

I look at Rosie, expecting her to shoulder her pack and lead the way like she always has. But Maddie's kidnapping has really shaken her. I have to get her to snap out of it.

"Rosie, do you think we have everything we need to make it to Chicago?" I ask.

"Everything except Maddie," she says. Apparently snapping out isn't going to be happening right this second.

"And food," Ryan adds.

Everyone is looking at me, like I should know what to do.

So I do the only thing I can think of: I pull on my pack, pick up my compass, say, "Chicago, here we come," and start walking. "We'll look for food as we go."

Except for occasional "You okay?" "Mm-hmm"–type exchanges, we spend the next four hours walking in silence, which isn't my natural habitat. (Of course, neither is Outside. Until recently my idea of being in nature was to sit next to a window. With a sweater on.)

Above us the sky hunches over the barren landscape like an old man over a checkerboard, gray, wary, and slightly unkempt. The air is warm, thick, and dusty. In the distance I can make out sharp veins of lightning as the afternoon electrical storm looks for anchors on the cars and towers of Chicago.

These mini-typhoons usually last only an hour, but they've started happening a lot this time of year, and only around the city. At least once a month there's a story on the NewsServ about a typhoo-tourist who came from some faraway place and ended up fried to a tofurkey crisp by the storm. From my room at home I often watch the storms weaving tissues of light around buildings and cars and anything metal. According to Mr. Larson, our house-keeper, the view of them from the attic is "dazzling," but I'm not crazy about heights so I've never been up there. Mr. Larson is convinced the storms are generated by the government to keep people off the streets and make them easier to control. He says all the stories about typhoo-tourists getting zapped are planted and that no one has ever seen a body and that the storms are actually harm-less. He promised one day we'll sneak out together and go out in one.

I picture Mr. Larson, leaning against the counter in our big, green and white kitchen, reading aloud from the NewsServ, glasses perched on the end of his nose and the vest of his suit unbuttoned. Meanwhile, Mr. Peña, our cook, gets dinner ready. My chest feels a little tight and I wish I had more nails to bite.

I glance at my compass to check our direction. As Louisa's deep sigh reminds me, I've checked it approximately a hundred times already, but I just want to be sure.

We're now about fourteen miles from Chicago, but we could be hundreds considering how unpopulated it is out here. There's nothing, not a house, or a store, or a bush with berries on it, which is bad since we haven't eaten in hours, but good since we are trying to avoid being seen.

Although I'm not completely convinced it's working, this whole not-being-seen thing. Twice I could have sworn I saw eyes glittering between the branches on either side of us. I'm tempted to ask the others if they've noticed anything, but I don't want to seem (even more) paranoid.

Dr. King, whom my parents sent me to because they were concerned that I worry an unhealthy amount, says I have a propensity toward catastrophic thinking coupled with a robust imagination, which leads me to be hyper-interrogatory, particularly when stressed.

That means I ask a lot of questions, especially if I'm nervous.

According to her, I use questions the way a dolphin uses sonar signals, sending them out into the world and taking findings to chart a safe passage through an unknown landscape. (Which would have been more reassuring if all the dolphins hadn't died mysteriously after the Great Pacific Superstorm, but don't mention that to your parents because they will roll their eyes and say, "You are doing it again; please *just stop!*")

I am starting to suspect Dr. King is right because as the darkness gathers around us, every step I take seems to echo with questions. Or rather, one question: Why, out of all of us, would someone kidnap only Maddie?

Drew, for example, would be a way better target. He said his mother was "pretty important" in the government in a way that suggests *pretty* means *very*, so he would be useful to the Alliance.

Alonso's family moves around frequently because they own an air cargo company — an evil group could do *a lot* with one of those.

Rosie is from a family rich enough to buy her a whole forged identity and therefore likely to be willing to pay a lot to ransom her.

Louisa is the daughter of two very successful doctors who would be good for a free kidney transplant or general patching-up-after-an-intensive-battle kind of thing. I know I always feel more confident when I have a good supply of bandages and antiseptic around.

When Ryan described his house outside of Chicago, I immediately knew which one it was — the one environmental blogs referred to as being an ethical and environmental disaster. Ryan's father had bought the three mansions around it when the owners lost their fortunes and razed them to put in a *real* grass golf course for himself. With parents who are loaded and unpopular, he is an excellent target for kidnappers. They could probably even auction him off to the highest bidder.

The same is true of me — my parents, both defense lawyers, are rich in money and enemies. Not to mention they know a lot of bad guys' bad secrets.

But Maddie doesn't have money or status, or access to

organs, or blackmail material to offer. Her parents are both regular soldiers, and she was only at CMS because Louisa's parents faked her ID and paid for her. Of us all, she's worth the least from a kidnapping perspective. So why —

My head whips around at the sound of a branch moving. I peer into the gathering darkness, but if there's anything there, it's not visible.

I'll admit, there might be the slightest chance that I'm a tad hyper about the possibility of danger. I mean, it's not like we're wandering around the Settlement Lands or someplace like *that*. But besides the very real possibility that we're being pursued by enemy agents, I've also heard rumors about escaped zoo animals that have made the now-deserted suburbs their lairs, along with roving packs of rabid dogs, swarms of carnivorous killer bees, and off-gridders who are willing to do anything — and by that I mean *eat* anything — to survive. A group of seven kids would make a great dinner for a hungry —

Not seven, I remind myself. Six. Maddie's gone.

And that's when the answer to *Why Maddie and Maddie alone* comes to me, hitting me with such force it knocks my breath out.

I lose my footing for a second and fall against Louisa. "What's wrong?" she asks.

I gulp and shake my head. "Nothing."

I can't tell her. I can't tell any of them. Because if I'm wrong, it will upset them for no reason. And if I'm right —

If I'm right, then Maddie was taken *because* she isn't valuable. Because she's . . . expendable. As bait for us or a message to our parents, she is worth as much or more to the Alliance dead than alive. Which means if we can't find her in time, she won't just be gone. She'll be gone for goo —

Was that a growl?

My mouth goes dry and my heart starts to race.

I glance over my shoulder, trying to make it look super casual, as though I'm just checking out how the rest of the group is doing, and not looking for predators with a taste for human flesh.

Rosie and Drew are right behind me. Rosie is shuffling forward, her gaze on the ground, hard fists jammed into the pockets of her hoodie. Drew, stumbling aimlessly beside her, somehow manages to appear sort of frail despite being by far the tallest and most athletically built of all of us. I wish they looked a little more intimidating.

Alonso and Ryan are following them, talking in a subdued way, but at least they look like they're more than half-zombie. Alonso catches my eye and gives me a smile.

Behind them is . . . nothing.

So why won't the hairs on the back of my neck and arms stop tingling?

I face forward again, but then a sharp wail splits the air behind me. I turn just in time to see Drew's eyes roll back in his head. Clutching his shoulder, he staggers forward and sinks facedown, unconscious.

Chapter 2

Faster than you can say, *Everyoneonthegroundthere couldbemorepoisondarts!* Louisa streaks by me like a blond comet and is on her knees next to Drew's lifeless body. Rosie kneels beside her and together they turn him over so he's lying on his back.

His navy blue jacket has fallen open and there's a flower of blood blooming near his left shoulder.

"This is my fault," I gasp. "I knew someone was following us and I should have said something and then we could have prevented them firing their poison darts and what if it's fatal and —"

"Oh my god, Evelyn, *shut up!*" Louisa orders. She unbuttons the striped cotton shirt Drew is wearing and pulls aside the T-shirt he has on beneath it to reveal a large, angry gash. "This isn't a poison dart; it's a cut, and it looks like it happened a while ago."

Drew's eyes flutter. "With Maddie," he says, his voice like the painful rasp of an unused hinge. "When I . . . to stop them . . . car door . . . my shoulder . . ."

"You're going to be fine," Louisa says to him in a tone that is comforting and authoritative at once. I don't know if it's because she's heard her parents do it, but she seems to have this doctor thing down.

Even though she just yelled at me, it makes me feel better, too. If this happened to Drew when he was trying to save Maddie, then it's not the result of anyone shooting at us or trying to ambush us.

And we (probably) aren't being followed.

Louisa's taken Ryan's water bottle and dripped a bit into Drew's mouth, then put some on Drew's shoulder.

"Sorry," she says as he winces. She looks at me with an intensity I'm not used to but her voice is still calm and almost casual as she says, "You have the first aid kit we got at CMS for the camping trip, right?" I nod and she goes on. "Can you find something to clean this with and something to use as a bandage? I'll just cover it up and after some *rest*, he'll be good as new." I realize she's sending me a message, that this is more serious than she's letting on, and we need to stop moving.

I find gauze and tape in my backpack without looking (you never know when the power might go out and you'll have to be able to locate supplies in the dark). Then I try to match her tone as I say, "I was thinking this would be a good place to break for the night."

And it's true, if you like narrow paths between scraggly bushes in the middle of an unknown wasteland. But we don't have a lot of choices. We only have a little more than an hour until nightfall. Even though it's been hot all day, at this time of year the temperature can drop sharply — and fast. We need to set up a camp.

My stomach rumbles, reminding me that we also need to find food.

The others give me a look that says, *Have you lost your mind?* and I give them a look that says, *He needs to rest*, and Louisa gives all of us a look that says, *Oh my god, you guys, stop — he's noticing.*

Drew says, "No. No resting. We're going on," and tries to sit up.

The color drains from his face and Rosie has to catch him before he passes out again. She gently but firmly lowers him back to the ground. "Behave yourself. Don't make me hurt you," she jokes.

He gives her what you can tell he thinks is a grin. "You could try but yo*eeeesshhh*," he yelps as Louisa dabs the antiseptic on his gaping wound. His breathing is unsteady and I can see he's squeezing Rosie's hand in pain. He swallows hard, twice. There are beads of sweat on his forehead. "I'm serious," he says through clenched teeth. "We don't have time. Leave me. The rest of you go."

Next to me Alonso gives a bark of laughter. "Yeah, that's not going to happen."

"If you want to get rid of us, you're going to have to try harder," Ryan adds.

"Can we move him?" Alonso asks Louisa. "I think there's a building over there." And following his finger, I see a glint of light. Not from the hungry eyes of a bloodthirsty predator, either, but from what looks like a partially broken windowpane.

"I can walk fine," Drew says, which is completely untrue. Rosie shoulders his pack, Alonso and Ryan get on either side of him, and Louisa and I follow in case he pitches backward.

It's farther than it looks to the building. Before we reach it the dirt begins to give way to asphalt and the trees thin. Soon the trees are replaced by waist-high rusted metal posts planted in perfectly straight rows. Some of them have wires twisting out of holes near the top, and in the darkening twilight they cast long shadows, like the fingers of evil witches.

A chill creeps up my spine.

The posts march toward a tangle of immense pieces of metal jutting haphazardly from a crumbling concrete base. They are clearly the remains of what had once been a massive curved structure, like an altar or an oracle or one of those places that ancient people used to make pilgrimages to. It's silent in the way only a place without trees can be silent, but a gust of wind comes up then and it makes an eerie whining sound.

"Do you think this is some kind of cemetery?" Ryan asks in a hushed whisper. "Or, like, haunted?"

"No." I say it more out of hope than conviction. Also I feel like there's something familiar about the layout of the place, something I've seen in an old movie.

"A drive-in," Rosie announces, interrupting my thoughts. "That's what this was. People came to them to watch movies. All those poles had speakers on them and people parked next to them in their cars. My parents told me about them."

"You mean every one of those was *for a car?*" There is awe in Alonso's voice that I totally understand. The idea of this many people being able to afford the gas to drive cars, not to mention to drive them just to sit in them and watch a movie *outside* when a superstorm could strike at any minute, is incredible.

"No wonder there's no gas left now," Louisa says.

The reflection we'd seen came not from a windowpane,

but from a metal star that looks like it had once been part of a sign, dangling from the side of a building on the edge of the lot. "That must have been the snack bar," I say, remembering the movie I'd seen about a drive-in. In it the people had parked and eaten pizza and drunk grape soda.

I really wish I hadn't retained that detail because it makes my stomach feel even hollower. When was the last time we ate? Yesterday?

Like he's reading my thoughts, Alonso says, "I think I saw some berry bushes on our way over here. Once we get the patient settled, we can go look."

We cross the rest of the way to the building, hurrying because the wind is picking up and making more of those eerie howling noises.

There's no door on the building, just a double metal frame where glass doors had once been. Inside, it's like time stood still. There's a beige counter with red-vinyl-topped stools in front of it. Over the counter hangs a sign offering the World Famous StarBrite Cinema All Beef Burger Deluxe (w/All the Fixin's!) for only $53.00 and

the Light Up Your Night Ice Cream Sundae with choco-
late sauce, nuts, whipped cream —

I have to stop reading. It's too painful. If you could even
get your hands on actual meat these days, a burger would
easily be five times that much, and even though I can't
imagine what a Fixin' is, I am positive that I would like it.

I bet none of us have ever had whipped cream.

All the windows have been boarded up, so even though
it's only dusk outside it's pretty dark in here. Rosie and I
turn on our flashlights. Dr. Louisa uses the sleeve of her
hoodie to dust off the counter and has Alonso and Ryan
stretch Drew out on it. Since I'm the one who can find
all the supplies in my backpack the quickest, we decide
I'll stay and assist while the others go look for food.

As I watch them emptying out their packs in antici-
pation of finding something, I can't help thinking of the
last time we separated this way. It was when Maddie and
Drew went looking for food, and that didn't end well.

"Actually, someone should stay and stand guard,"
Rosie says, as if she'd been reading my mind. "Just — in
case there's some kind of situation." I nod. I personally

will feel much better knowing Rosie of all people is watching out for us.

There's an awkward moment right before Alonso and Ryan go outside, like we're all wondering if something will happen. The wind howls again, bringing a chilly gust that smells of night into the building. It reminds us we don't have any time to waste.

As soon as the others are gone, Louisa hops into action. "We're going to need to clean the cut, then dry it and seal it up," she says, sounding like she knows what she's doing.

I hold her flashlight in the crook of my neck and my flashlight in my left hand. With my free hand, I pass her things when she asks for them. Water bottle. Antiseptic again. More gauze.

"Do you have anything like tweezers?" she asks.

I'm about to shake my head when I remember the Alliance prison camp we accidentally broke into three — can it really be only *three*? — days ago. I fish in my bag and pull out the staple remover. "Will this work?" I ask, holding it up.

28

She takes it. "Perfect." She begins plucking tiny pieces of gravel out of Drew's arm. He winces in pain, but she's quick. Without taking her eyes off her task, she says, "I'm sorry, about before. When I yelled at you?"

"That's okay. I understand."

"I think I was a little jealous. Of you and Maddie. The way you became friends at school. And so when I was upset, I took it out on you."

This surprises me. "But Maddie is your best friend, no question."

"I know." She nods. "But as soon as we got to CMS, it was like she changed." She lets out a big breath. "Or maybe it was me that changed. Anyway, she was smart to become friends with you. And I'm glad you ask all those questions."

"That's impossible. No one is glad I ask so many questions."

Her hands don't stop moving but she shoots me a sly, sideways glance. "I think Alonso is. At least based on the way he looks at you."

"What?" I ask, almost dropping the flashlight that's balanced in the crook of my neck. As far as I can tell, Alonso looks at me the same way he looks at everything and everyone else.

"With those big brown puppy-dog eyes like —"

"I don't know what you're talking about," I say, bending my head meaningfully toward Drew in the universal signal of *I will kill you if you bring this up in front of a boy.*

But Louisa just smiles innocently at Drew's wound and says, "Evelyn, please hold that light steady." Then the smile fades and her hands stop moving and she looks up at me. "I'm serious. I'm glad you are the way you are. If anyone can find her, it's you. I know it. Liquid skin."

It takes me a moment to realize she's changed topics. I hand her the little bottle of wound sealant and watch as she daubs it on expertly. It's like she's a whole different person, more serious and focused than I've ever seen her before.

"Did you watch your parents at work a lot?" I ask.

She tucks a stray piece of blond hair behind her ear. "Not really. They would have liked me to, I think, but I wasn't that interested. I — I never thought I was cut out to be a doctor. Not smart enough."

"Are you kidding? You're amazing," I tell her.

"When I was little I used to get hurt on the playground a lot, swinging from the bars and stuff. They were always patching me up, and I guess I picked up more than I thought I did. There." She takes a step back. "That should stop the bleeding."

I glance at the wound and it looks a million times better. You would have thought a real doctor did it. Drew seems to have fallen asleep at some point but it's clear he's going to be fine by the morning.

We turn off our flashlights to save the batteries, move a little farther down the counter, and each take a stool. It's almost completely dark, the open door a silvery outline, the corners of the room pitch-black. Even though Louisa is sitting only a foot from me, she's nearly invisible.

The stools are cracked on the tops but they're still sitable and they spin around. I bet it was super fun to come here with your friends.

I say, "What are you going to have? I'm thinking of a burger with all the fixin's."

"Oh heavens no, not for me. I'm dieting for my vay-cay," Louisa says, hamming it up. I wonder what it was like to live in a time when there was so much food some people went on diets. "My family and I are going on a luxury cruise around the Greek Isles and I want to look good in my bikini." Her stool squeaks as she moves from side to side. "What were fixin's, anyway?"

"Something incredibly delicious," I assure her.

"Wait — you don't know? I thought you knew everything."

"Ha-ha."

"Seriously, how come you know so much about almost any topic?" she asks. "Like about the government and the Alliance and stuff? Is that from your parents?"

Even though it's dark, I roll my eyes. "No way. My parents never tell me anything about what's going on in the world. They like to pretend everything is perfect and everything is going to be okay. They're all, 'Don't worry about it, Evelyn; that wasn't an explosion in Cleveland. I don't know where you heard that; don't you have homework?'" I say, imitating my mother's voice. "Which of course just makes me more curious. Even just *skimming* the NewsServs it's clear that everything is NOT okay. How can everything be okay when it's started snowing every other month and farmers can't grow food? Or when California hasn't had power in two years or —"

I realize Louisa's gone really quiet. "Never mind," I say.

"I was just thinking," she says. "My parents are like your parents. They never tell me anything bad and they always say everything is going to be okay but I — I always just believe they're right. Now —" Her lip trembles and I make out a flash of movement as her fingers go to her throat. "Now I'm not sure. They said not to worry and I didn't. I just took everything for granted. I didn't realize how easy it was for it to all disappear."

I know that the place on her neck she's touching is where she used to have a gold locket that got lost when we were escaping from CMS. But I think she must be thinking of Maddie, too. I'm sure of it when she says,

"When we first got to school and I liked it and she hated it, there were a few nights where I got into bed and she and I weren't speaking. You know that kind of silence? I thought it was awful. But now — now I'd trade anything for that. Because not having her here, not knowing what's happening to her, that is really awful. You're positive we can get her back, aren't you?"

"We have to," I say.

"Thank you," Louisa says. "You made me feel much better."

Which is good. It's what I wanted to do. So why do I feel worse?

Rosie pokes her head through one of the empty doors. "The guys just whistled for help carrying some stuff. I'll be right back. Don't get into trouble."

"Aye, aye, Officer Rosie," I say, glad to be distracted.

Louisa's stomach rumbles and she laughs. "Not a moment too soon. I just realized I'm starving. I must be feeling better."

"Or else *Ryan* is rubbing off on you."

She says, "Shut up!" and points furiously at Drew. I start to laugh and she starts to laugh and it feels so good, almost better than food.

We're still laughing when we hear the heavy footsteps of the food-laden boys approaching the building.

"Finally," Louisa says playfully as they get to the door, and one of them shines a flashlight beam in our faces.

We've draped ourselves over the counter, pretending to be passed out with hunger. "Food . . . please . . . help us . . ." Louisa squeaks piteously, and we're both still laughing when a voice we've never heard before speaks.

"Stand up and put your hands over your head or your friend gets it," the voice says.

And someone pushes Rosie, in a headlock, into the edge of the beam of light.

Chapter 3

This is bad. If I'd been holding a Least Likely to Be Caught in a Headlock contest, Rosie would have been hands-down winner. So whoever did this is good.

Well trained.

Professional.

Or at least that is what I assume until the voice behind the flashlight says, "Who are you?"

Because if they don't know who we are, that means they aren't Alliance agents sent to bring us back to CMS. But then —

"Who are *you*?" I demand.

"I asked you first," the voice behind the flashlight snaps. Which is true, but not something a professional grown-up would say. "And we have your friend."

The beam moves slightly. For the first time I can see the person who's holding Rosie. It's a girl, and she looks unkempt and kind of wild, but not much older than we are.

I squint and try to see the person holding the light. It's a boy, maybe a year older than us, and it looks like he has a bandage covering one eye. My arms start to come down and he barks, "Keep them up. Believe me, you don't want to mess with us."

Somehow, their just being kids and still managing to sneak up on Rosie is even more disturbing than if they were pros. I agree and clamp my hands over my ponytail. I say, "We're runaways from an Alliance school."

"Don't look like fliers," the one-eyed boy says. "Which school? I know them all, so don't think of lying."

I file that word, "fliers," away.

Louisa answers, "Country Manor School."

"Never heard of Country Manor School," he says impatiently. "Where is it?"

"We don't know. It's — in a secret place," she falters.

I step in. "North of here about two days."

"Sure." One Eye gives a snort and the flashlight dips as he bends and picks up one of our backpacks. He spills the contents on the ground and starts kicking through them. He moves to the next pack, repeats the process. Only this time something interests him. He stops, bends sideways to grab it for a closer look.

He stands up and says, "That's it — get rid of their friend."

What?!?

"Troy, I'm not sure —" the girl says.

"Look what they have," he interrupts, tossing a jacket toward her. As the light catches it, I realize it's one of the Alliance uniforms Drew and Rosie stole when we broke into the prison camp. "I told you they were Alliance."

This is not good.

"No, we *stole* that," I tell them. My voice sounds a little hysterical to my ears. "To escape from a prison camp."

"I thought you said you were at a school," the girl says. Her tone is a lot cooler than it had been. Murderously cool.

"We were, but while we were escaping we ended up in an Alliance prison, and in order to get out —" I stop trying to explain. The more I say, the more far-fetched it sounds. I have to try something else. "Look, you just dumped our packs. We don't have any food, do we? If we worked for the Alliance, if we weren't really runaways, we'd have food, right?"

One Eye gives another snort. "You could have hidden it."

The girl with her arm around Rosie hasn't moved. Now she says, "They don't have badges, Troy, or ID bracelets. They might be telling the truth."

"Isn't that what they would do? Send them without badges or IDs to make them look desperate?"

"And they stuck to back paths," she goes on.

"That's precisely how they would act. Undercover 101."

"You were following us?" I breathe out with disbelief. I'd been right! Someone *was* trailing us.

"All day," the boy called Troy answers. There's a sneer in his voice as he adds, "And you didn't even know it."

"If they are working undercover, they're really bad at it," the girl says thoughtfully.

"That's what they want you to believe. It could be a trick."

I sense that, in other circumstances, Troy and I might have a lot in common.

I say, "Who are you hiding from? The people in the black trucks?"

There's a subtle shift in the air, nothing I can name, but suddenly Troy and the girl both seem tenser. Troy says something that sounds like "Felix" and at the same time the girl snaps, "What do you know about those?"

"Some people in a black truck took our friend Maddie," Louisa tells them. "Madeleine Frye. Have you seen her?"

"Where?" the boy demands, and at the same time the girl says, "When?"

I look at the shadowy forms behind the light. "Earlier today. About ten miles from here. Who are they?"

The boy and girl exchange a glance. The girl says, "We don't know your friend."

"But you know the people in the black truck," I confirm. I'm convinced they have intel that could help us. But not while the girl is holding Rosie by the neck.

"Keep your hands up," Troy shouts at me.

That's what gives me my idea. "Where did you run away from?" I ask.

The girl hesitates.

I try another tactic. "Did you come out of Chicago by the lake or along the highway?"

"Don't tell them anything," Troy yells at the girl. He seems even more wary than before.

"But, Troy, I think they're telling the tr —"

"And stop using my name. Don't you see what they're doing? They're trying to turn us against each other."

Louisa shoots me a glance that says, *What are you doing behind your back?* and I lean forward slightly so she can see. She frowns but then gets it and her face softens.

Luckily our captors don't seem to notice. "They just want to win your trust," Troy goes on. "Once they do, they'll throw you in a Rover and take you back."

"You're being irrational," the girl says.

Troy makes a sound like a growl. "Irrational? I'm not going back to Phoenix. I won't be a slave. I'll do whatever it takes to keep from going back."

I've been trying to draw as little attention to myself as possible but I have to ask, "Who is Phoenix? Is that who the people in the black trucks work for?"

The light, which had shifted slightly while they argued, swings back to me. "Who's Phoenix?" Troy repeats with a high-pitched laugh. "Look at that, sis. See how well trained they are? Who's Phoenix, she asks."

"Stop it, Troy," the girl says. And then to me, "Ignore my brother; he's under a lot of stress."

"I won't go!" he says, swinging the light off of me just enough so I can pass the rubber band I freed from my hair to Louisa. "I won't let them take me back!" he repeats, staring at us with a mad glitter in his one eye.

"Now," I whisper, and Louisa, with her expert aim, shoots the rubber band at it.

"They stabbed me!" he yells, covering his eye with his hand. The flashlight falls to the ground and the building goes completely dark.

The girl shrieks, "What have you done?" and Rosie's voice from somewhere in front of us says, "Don't even think about it," and there's a grunt and a scuffle and another grunt. I can't believe I left my night-vision goggles at CMS. In the six and a half seconds it takes me to reach for my flashlight and get it on, Rosie has gotten her arm around the guy's neck and Louisa has her hands around the girl's ankle and she's lying on the ground where she fell when she tried to run away.

"Now *you* answer questions," Rosie says to them, pushing the boy onto the floor and clamping a hand on his shoulder.

Louisa lets the girl turn around so the brother and sister are sitting next to each other, and we get a good look at them for the first time. Their faces are red, like they have been sunburned, but that could just be from the fighting. The boy's hair is matted down and the girl's looks like she hasn't washed it in a few days and they both have oddly short, uneven bangs. They are both wearing what appear to be inside-out hoodies and cargo pants.

"I know you're Troy," I say to the boy. "What's your name?" I ask the girl.

"Don't answer," Troy tells her. "Don't answer any questions under duress."

"You're not under duress," I say. "You can leave anytime." Rosie frowns at me but it's true. We're not jailors.

"My name is Helen," the girl says. And she starts to cry. "This is all a stupid miscalibration." As Helen pulls the sleeve of her hoodie over her hand and uses it to dry her eyes, I resist the urge to ask if she means "miscalculation." "My brother and I — you're right." She looks at me. "We're on the run from a place in Chicago. We grew up in Wisconsin but our parents, well, they're not around. We've been on our own for a while. But it's tough, you know. We got arrested for shoplifting a few times. The last time, Troy . . . He . . . hit the police officer. Beat him up pretty good. Or bad, depending on which side you're on. We ran away, but they found us."

"Rovers," Troy says, but it seems like his mind is partially somewhere else.

"That's what those black trucks are called. Rovers," Helen supplies. "That's what we were picked up in. Then they loaded us into a bus with the windows blacked out and drove us for hours. There were three of us, me and Troy and one other guy." She pauses and licks her lips. "We thought for sure we were going to a prison camp somewhere far away. But instead they took us to a school. Like a reform school but kind of *nice*."

"'You've been chosen,'" Troy says in a deep voice different from his own, and I realize he's quoting someone. Probably Phoenix. "'You are being given a second chance. Your record will be wiped clean and you will become part of an elite group. You are the lucky few, the proud.'" He shakes himself and repeats, "Chosen."

"At the beginning we did feel lucky," Helen says. "The classes were cool, not boring like regular school. And there were clean beds and clothes and lots of food."

"All courtesy of your friends in the Alliance," Troy says.

"Wait." I sit forward. "It was an Alliance school? In Chicago?"

"That's what we figured out." Helen nods vigorously. "That's why we escaped."

One thing about being suspicious of everything everyone says is when you hear the truth, it sounds — strange. Unfamiliar. But distinct. That's how Helen sounds now.

I of all people shouldn't be surprised that there's an Alliance facility in the middle of Chicago, but it's still kind of staggering. Which is why it takes me a second to see what this means: this could be where Maddie is. If we find the school, we could find her. "Where exactly is this place?" I ask.

"They have showers, too," Troy says, completely ignoring me. I want to break in but it's like he's somewhere else. His head is tilted and his one eye is squarely focused on his hands. "But they don't work. You can't get clean. It's in your hair and your clothes and your eyes. No matter what you do, you always smell like *it*. Even now I smell it." He gazes around at us, and his eye has a kind of strange sheen.

"That's enough, Troy," Helen says, wrapping her fingers around his forearm to calm him.

46

His hands clutch his ears. "And the noise. They shriek when you do it, like you're stealing their souls," he says as though he hasn't heard her.

"Snap out of it, Troy!" she says sharply.

This time he does. His hands drop and his eye focuses on me and he looks dead serious. "Look for the big lie —"

"Silence!" Helen barks, and his mouth shuts. She kneels in front of him and takes him by the shoulders. "Look at me. You need to stop talking. Stop scaring these people. You don't want to scare them with your *made-up* stories, do you?"

"What?" I ask, trying to get his attention back. "What big lie?"

He looks at me, and I could swear I read disappointment in his expression. "No, *I told you,* not lie —" I see Helen's knuckles whiten as she tightens her grip on his shoulders and he falls silent. His eye is glued to her face as though he's mesmerized. When he talks next his voice is flat, affectless. "Nothing. I was making it up. Sometimes I — my mind gets mixed up." Helen nods and lets go of his shoulders.

She sits back down and faces us. "You shouldn't take what Troy says seriously. My brother isn't well. He gets started on a train of thought and then he has these hallucinations and they seem so real to him he believes they're true."

"But the school is real," I argue. "You said so. Can you describe where it is? The street, anything?"

"Not really," Helen says. She's not meeting my eyes and the strange sound of truth is gone. "The bus pulled into, like, a garage or something and we went inside and we didn't get a chance to see anything outside. It was always dark or we were in class."

"How about when you escaped? How did you get out?"

"Shoot," Troy says with a little laugh. "It was the only way. They never even thought of it."

Helen goes completely still for one full second; then she laughs but not for real, like she's forcing herself to do it. "Shoot, it was hard, the way we did it," she says, and it sounds completely fake.

She takes a deep breath and says, "What we did was, we waited until dark and then climbed down the side of the building with ropes, and then there was a wall and a fence. And after that we were just running as hard as we could."

I'm almost positive that she is lying but I want to be sure. "What was the building made of?"

Her eyes go left, then come back to me. "Cinderblocks," she says. Which is what the snack bar we're sitting in is made of. "Look, I'm sorry we can't help you find your friend but I really don't know where the building is or what it looked like or anything."

"Do you know in what direction you ran when you left?"

"Sure." Helen stares at me hard. "The direction that didn't have any cops in it."

"She's asking too many questions," Troy says to Helen. "I don't like all the questions. I want to go."

"Trust me," she tells him.

He's in the middle of nodding when he sits up straighter, a hunting dog on a scent. His head whips around toward the door and he says, "Who's coming? Someone's coming!" as Alonso and Ryan walk through it.

For a moment everyone is frozen, caught like those birds you used to see in trees after flash ice storms.

Then Ryan slides his hands from the pockets of his parka to the straps of his backpack and says, "How come you didn't tell us you'd invited company for dinner?"

"Yeah," Alonso agrees, setting down a bucket they'd managed to find somewhere that is full of delicious-looking berries. "We would have shopped for something special." They're being casual but they've also just assumed fighting stances.

"This is Helen and her brother, Troy," I tell them so they know we're okay.

Helen gives Alonso a nice smile. "And don't worry about dinner; we were just going. We don't have time to waste."

I start to ask if they're sure — I mean, they still might share something that could help us — but Rosie's look of relief stops me. I say, "Good luck," instead.

"Thanks." Helen stands up. "And good luck to you finding your friend. Marley."

"Maddie," Louisa corrects her.

"Right."

Troy gets up, too, and starts to turn toward the door. His sister gives him a look that is apparently an instruction to stay put. He stands there, hands dangling at his sides.

Helen comes over and hugs me and hugs Louisa. Then she offers her hand to Rosie. "No hard feelings."

"Just hard knocks," Rosie says, which must be some kind of warrior slogan because Helen smiles. The moment Helen has Rosie's hand in hers, she turns and yells, "Now!" at Troy.

Troy rushes Alonso, pushes him aside, grabs the full bucket of berries, and takes off. Helen moves backward toward the door holding a knife in front of her, clearly willing to use it if she has to.

She dips down to grab the Alliance uniform jacket and stops at the door. Light flashes off the edge of the blade. "If you know what's good for you, you'll forget you ever laid eyes on us, and you'll hope we do the same." She steps backward over the empty doorframe, turns to the right, and is swallowed up into the night.

Along with all our food.

Chapter 4

"I'm going after her," Rosie says, starting for the door.

Ryan steps in front of the door to stop her from leaving. "It's not worth it."

"She stole our dinner."

"Not really," he says. "Although you'd think they would have said something about hating to eat and run."

"Only it would have had to be run and eat," Drew points out from the stool he's been sitting on.

"He's *baaaaaaaaaaaaack!*" Alonso announces, heading toward Drew and giving him a one-armed hug. "How are you feeling, old man?"

Drew winces a little but he looks a lot better. "Like a black military vehicle slammed into my shoulder but then I had an expert doctor look after it."

Rosie turns around, hands curled into fists on her hips, looking fierce. "How can you joke about this? We should be out there, after her."

Drew pushes himself off the stool. "It's pitch-dark out there; there's no way anyone could find her," he says. "Even you."

Rosie's scowl goes from Roiling Boil to Simmer, and her fists uncurl.

"What did you mean about her not really stealing our dinner?" Louisa asks.

Ryan bends to set down his pack and opens it. "The berries they took were the ones we were keeping separate because we weren't sure if they were poisonous or not." He pulls out a bag, unties the top, and pours at least three pounds of deep blue berries onto the counter. "We still have these."

"Feel free to tell us how quietly brilliant we are," Alonso suggests.

"Not me," Ryan says. "My brilliance isn't quiet at all."

The mood in the snack bar lifts, and lifts more when Alonso produces five handfuls of fuzzy green lumps from his pack. "And nuts. We think they're some kind of almonds but we're not sure. Ryan ate one and he's fine."

Ryan blows on his fingernails and pretends to polish them on his shoulder. "You got that right," he says. "That's Mr. Fine to you."

Boys are really strange.

We divide up the food evenly and start eating. I put a berry in my mouth and bite down and it explodes with a burst of tart juice on my tongue. I eat another as I peel off the green skin of one of the nuts and edge the tip of my CMS-issued knife in the crack to pry it open. It takes work but the nut inside is crunchy with a taste somewhere between an almond and a peanut.

Maybe it's because I'm starving, but I think these are probably the best nuts and berries I have ever eaten in my life, possibly the best ones in the world. For five minutes the only noise in the snack bar is the sound of shells cracking open.

Until Louisa says, "I wish they'd taken me, too." She puts down her knife and pushes away the rest of her nuts.

I'm sitting next to her, so I can hear the trembling i[n] voice.

"Who?" I ask, setting down my knife and tur[n] toward her.

"The people in the — what did Helen and Troy it? — Rover. The people who took Maddie." She lo[oks] around at all of us and there are tears in the corners [of] her eyes. I slide off my stool and give her a hug.

"I hate thinking of her there alone," she says into m[y] shoulder. "Why did they take only *her*?"

My throat feels like it's closing up.

Louisa pulls away from me but keeps hold of my wrist as she repeats, "Why?"

I can't move. I can't breathe. I can't tell them.

"Maybe because she's the smallest," Ryan says after a moment.

"That would make her the easiest to control," Alonso confirms. "That makes sense."

"And to feed," Rosie points out. She brushes the shells from her hands and touches Louisa lightly on the arm.

"Seriously, what if they'd taken Ryan?" Alonso puts

in then. "They'd waste all their ransom money on food."
I don't know what Louisa meant before about how he
looks at me, but the way he's looking at her now, like it
matters to him that she feels better, is really nice.

And it's successful. She relaxes the hold on my wrist
and gives a little smile and says, "I guess."

Drew sits up straighter. "The truth is, we might not
know why. But at least now we have some idea of who
took her, and where. Right, Evelyn?"

I discover I've been holding my breath. "Right," I say.
"We have something to go on."

Disaster is averted. Eating recommences. Boys are
strange but at this moment I am really glad they're here.

We are filling Alonso and Ryan in on what Helen
and Troy told us when there's a tapping on the boards
over one of the windows.

Followed by a low moaning.

Instinctively, we all turn off our flashlights. What
you can't see, you can't shoot.

"That's just wind," Rosie says, but next to me I feel
her tense. My palms get clammy.

Something thuds on the roof of the building, and there's a sound like feet skittering over it.

"What's that?" I whisper to Rosie in the dark, my heart racing.

"Tree branches?" she whispers back, not sounding completely sure.

That's when a voice outside demands, "Who?"

I jump to my feet, panting. "That is not the wind; that is someone —"

"*Who who,*" the voice calls again. An owl. It's an owl.

Everyone else starts to laugh. But it takes some time for the "All clear, just nature" message to get from my brain to my heart, which continues running a race in my chest. Our flashlights click back on.

Drew pulls himself to his feet. "Look, I'm feeling much better. This place is creepy and I think we should keep moving."

"Yeah, I wouldn't mind putting some distance between us and our lovely visitors," Alonso says.

The speed with which everyone else leaps up and starts shoving things in their packs shows how much they agree.

We skirt the edge of the pavement toward a driveway Ryan and Alonso saw before, which we're pretty sure must lead to the highway. It's long past seven thirty, which means long past curfew, but since it's night we decide to risk walking on the road where we'll make better time. The chances of there being anyone driving, with the current price of gas, is remote. And even if there is someone, we'll hear their engine or see their lights before they can see us in the dark.

Drew and his personal physician lead the way, with Ryan and Alonso behind them. Rosie hangs back to walk next to me.

"Do you really think Maddie is in that place that Helen and Troy came from?" she asks.

"It sounds like she was picked up by the same people, and the tire tracks headed to Chicago," I say. Our breaths are making little clouds in the cool air. "It's a good place to start. Why?"

"I don't know." Rosie kicks a stone from the road. "I thought Helen was mostly talking to stall until Alonso and Ryan came back with the food once you pointed out we didn't have any."

My fingers tighten around the straps of my backpack. "I shouldn't have done that. I was just worried they were going to hurt you."

Rosie pats me on the arm. "Believe me, I'm not complaining. You handled that great."

"Really?" I say. I instantly feel a thousand times better.

"Yeah." She purses her lips. "Although I do think it's a bit funny that you can talk down two crazy hostage takers and save my life, but you're afraid of an owl."

"I didn't know it was an owl!" I object. "Besides, you were scared, too."

"Nuh-uh," Rosie says.

"Uh-huh," I reply.

"I'll accept 'startled' over 'scared,'" Rosie says, like she's bargaining.

"Done," I tell her.

We both laugh and I have to admit, despite everything that is going on, it feels really nice. For a moment I have this powerful sense that even though I'm not sure how or where or when, working together we *will* find Maddie.

"Assuming the school is real," Rosie goes on, "how do we find it?"

"Even though Helen was lying, I have the impression that they told us more than they meant to." I try to explain what I mean. "When Troy talked about the Phoenix, and the smells and sound, that all seemed completely real."

"Helen said he made it all up," Rosie points out.

"Which practically guarantees that it's true," I say. I am starting to get excited. "And it happened again when I asked Troy how they escaped and he said, 'Shoot.' She tried to cover it up. Why would she have done that if it wasn't true?"

"But if they have a gun, why didn't they use it on us?" Rosie asks.

She's right. "I don't know." And yet I can't help thinking there's something there. "Do you know that feeling when you're close to uncovering an answer or solving a problem, but you can't quite touch it?"

Rosie nods slowly. "I do. Remember when we were in that prison camp?"

I give her a look. "No, I'm afraid I have totally forgotten about the time when we broke into a prison camp. What was it, thirty-six hours ago?"

She makes a face at me. "I'm serious. When we were there, I — I felt like I was close to finding my sister, Wren. Like maybe if I stayed, I could figure out what happened to her after Ivan betrayed her, where she ended up. Is that the same?"

"No," I say. "That's much worse." And then it hits me just how bad. I turn toward her. "You gave up that chance to save the rest of us."

She shrugs, not meeting my eyes. "What choice did I have? You would never have gotten anywhere without me." Her tone is light but I can tell it hurts. "Of course, maybe you would have been better off. Maybe then Maddie would still be here."

I stop walking and she stops, too, and turns to face me. "You have to cut that out." I tell her. "There was nothing you could have done to keep Maddie from being kidnapped. Whoever took her knew who she was and knew what they were doing. The only thing that could have gone differently was that you could have gotten hurt as well as Drew. Is that what you want?"

She stares at me wide-eyed and I realize everyone else has stopped in the middle of the road and is staring at me, too. Silence falls hard and heavy.

"She's right," Louisa says, coming to stand next to Rosie. "There was nothing you could do."

"Maddie wouldn't want you to beat yourself up," I point out.

Rosie flips her hand in the air, brushing this aside. "People always say that."

That makes me angry — I am not *people* — and maybe that's why I say, "In this case it happens to be true. Maddie wouldn't want you to be throwing a pity party for yourself because you lost her the same way you lost Wren." I hear Rosie's sharp intake of breath but I don't stop. "She would want you to focus on what needs to happen next, not what happened before. She'd want you, the strongest leader in our group, to help find her. And if we can find Maddie, we can find your sister."

Rosie's jaw is tight and she takes three breaths before she says, "Do you really think so? Do you really think that's true?"

"I do," I say. If I'm not going to mention that I think Maddie might be (as good as) dead, there's no reason to mention I have no idea how to find Wren.

A jagged bolt of lightning splits the sky. Oh great. At least now I know what the heavens think of my new lying habit.

"That's quite an omen," Alonso says.

"Yeah, an omen that we should find shelter," Rosie answers, sounding like her old self, and I get a warm feeling in my chest. "It's about to pour."

The sky opens up when we're near an abandoned strip mall by the side of the road. It's raining so hard that we're all soaked by the time we're beneath the overhang. Water is sluicing down my back in rivers.

The doors and windows of the stores have been boarded over. On the third door we try, a piece of plywood gives with a little pulling. Our entrance stirs up dust and our flashlight beams crisscross as we step inside.

It takes a moment to understand that we're surrounded.

"Leprechauns?" Louisa says. She bends close to one of the cardboard cutouts of a smiling man in a matching green top hat and suit.

Ryan shines his light on the ground. "And four-leaf clovers. Must be our lucky day."

Rosie crouches to pick up a rectangle of paper. "'Frankly Parties,'" she reads from the card. "'Making life more fun for Greater Chicago for fifty years.'" She lets the card flutter back to the floor. "I guess the market for fun isn't what it once was."

"I'm not sure I would ever have thought this was fun." Drew holds up an object that appears to be a moldy hamster in a Santa outfit.

I'd love to take off my sodden boots but the floor is thick with the leftovers of "fun." There's a torn HAPPY

3RD BIRTH — banner and another banner that proclaims, VELCOME TO SPOOKSYLVANIA. A pirate glares out from a tattered paper plate and part of a shiny blue balloon offers me — GRATULATIONS ON YOUR NEW BA —. There are two rows of what had been shelves running the length of the store, but they've been dismantled. One wall has a peeling paint mural of Santa in his sleigh flying over a landscape across which the Easter Bunny is making tracks with a basket of brightly colored eggs pursued by a ghost, a witch, and a mummy.

My foot brushes something and there's a weird bleating noise that I think is supposed to be music and a voice saying, "Show me the money, show me the money." I bend down and see that the noise is coming from inside a card that reads *For my beloved Grampa* on the front.

"A classic," Alonso says, squelching up beside me. "Bet it works every time."

"Check it out," Ryan calls from the far corner of the store. Five flashlight beams converge on him. He's standing under a thatched roof with the sign TIKI TIME! dangling from it. The remnants of a poster showing a turquoise ocean lapping at white sand under a cloudless sky are still plastered to the wall, flanked by two dust-covered plastic palm trees.

"Welcome to my surf shack," Ryan says. "I invite you all to camp out with me on the beach."

"I call ocean view," Alonso says and plops his stuff down opposite the poster.

We all pull off our packs. Fortunately, even though we're soaked, we discover that our sleeping bags managed to stay relatively dry. Of course, since we're sleeping in wet clothes, that matters less, but hopefully our body heat will dry them by the morning.

"It's weird to think people felt like they had to buy all this stuff just to have a good time," Louisa says, sitting down on her sleeping bag and toweling her hair with her spare T-shirt. "From what I remember before the War and the way my parents describe things, life was pretty great."

"Look at this," Rosie says, holding up a satin ribbon that has SWEET SIXTEEN PRINCESS written on it in glitter. She fingers the lettering. "Can you imagine?"

We all shake our heads. That sash certainly wouldn't

go with the military uniform we'll all be wearing on our sixteenth birthdays.

Ryan's eyes get big. "This store must have been out of business for a *long* time. The mandatory enlistment age was lowered to fifteen, what, four years ago?"

"Five," Alonso corrects him.

Sometimes when I think about what it must have been like before the War, I can't understand why it happened. I mean, even with the superstorms, people got to have jobs they chose, and kids didn't have to enlist in the army. I would give anything to be able to stay in school until my *eighteenth* birthday; people in those days could go to school until they were in their *twenties*. How much they must have known. How many questions they had gotten the answers to.

I feel a pang of envy for the girl who would have gotten to be a sweet sixteen princess. I wonder if she knew how lucky she was.

I pull myself out of my thoughts as Louisa says, "I think my favorite holiday is my birthday. My parents always take the day off from work and we do something as a family." She touches the place where her missing locket would be.

"Mine's Thanksgiving." Ryan rubs his stomach. "No question. I love soysausage stuffing."

"What about you, Rosie?" Louisa asks. "What's your favorite holiday? The first day of hunting season?"

"Halloween," Rosie answers right off.

"Yeah, the candy is awesome," Ryan agrees.

"Not because of the candy." She gives a casual shrug of one shoulder, says "I like dressing up," and glares around the circle at us as if defying us to find anything wrong with that.

I almost choke to keep from laughing, and Louisa is pressing her lips together so hard she's turning pink. It's hard to imagine no-nonsense Rosie having fun putting on a costume.

"What?" Rosie demands.

"Nothing," I say really fast because I don't want her to hurt me. "It's just a surprise."

She studies me to make sure I'm not making fun of her, then switches to studying the end of her ponytail.

"I'm the same thing every year. And don't even ask because I'm not telling."

"No fair!" Louisa cries.

Drew says, "Is it a ninja warrior? Because I could see you rocking that."

"No." Rosie keeps looking at her ponytail but I can see that she's smiling.

"My favorite is the Fourth of July," Drew says. "It's the one day my mom always takes off, and we have a barbecue. No one in the world makes better barbecue poultofu than my mother. It's" — he pantomimes licking his fingers — "ambrosia."

"Is it me, or do boys only think about food?" Rosie asks Louisa and me.

"They only think about food," Louisa confirms, then turns to Alonso. She's taken her hair out of its rubber band and is running her fingers through it, and she looks really pretty. "Let me guess. You like Easter because of the chocoveg bunnies."

He gives her a really cute smile and says, like he's sorry to disappoint her, "Yeah, I don't really do the whole holiday thing." His tone is easy, but his posture is rigid and he seems very uncomfortable.

I feel bad that we teased him. "I agree," I say. "Holidays are just corporate fabrications designed to sedate us so we don't see how horrible the world is."

Alonso turns and gives me a smile, too. "I knew someone would understand." I'm pretty sure that's not why he got so tense, but I'm not going to pry.

Plus, the way he is looking at me is making me feel — odd. But if this is what Louisa meant about him looking at me in some special way, I know she's wrong because it's nothing like the way he looked at her.

Ryan gives a big fake stretch and says, "Whew, somehow after that relaxing day of hanging around doing nothing and that huge delicious meal, I'm beat. I think I'll turn in."

"You sure you don't want to hit a few discos?" Alonso asks.

"You kids go on without me," Ryan tells him. "I want to get plenty of sleep for my early golf date."

We're all laughing at them as we tuck our packs under our sleeping bags to use for pillows. I've just settled into mine when Louisa says, "Evelyn, how far do you think we are from Chicago?"

I mentally review the map. "Four hours."

Rosie yawns. "If the slowpoke boys can keep up."

"Oh, them's fighting words," Drew says. "You better get a lot of sleep, miss, because you have a race on your hands."

One by one our flashlights go out and we get quiet. The space is filled with the sound of us shifting in our sleeping bags and the rain pouring down outside. Above me the spiky fronds of the fake palm tree stir gently in the wind that comes through the gap in the door planking.

As I lie there I think about my favorite holiday. It's not a holiday as much as the memory of a special day when I was much younger, back before the War started. Both my parents took off work and we went ice-skating outside. It snowed a little and the trees looked like they were frosted, and afterward they took me for real hot chocolate at a fancy restaurant and I sat between them and felt completely safe. Completely at home.

Four hours from Chicago, I'd said. And we are. But not four hours from home.

Chapter 5

The store is silent when my eyes open, and only the slightest hints of daylight filter inside.

Everyone else is still asleep but my mind has been restless all night, like a hamster in an old vid clip running endlessly on a wheel. Over and over, I see myself repeating back Troy's words, *What big lie?* then Troy's face filling with disappointment and him saying, *No, I told you, not lie —*

I told you.

Told me what?

I slip out of my sleeping bag, carefully lift my backpack, and go toward the front of the store. There's a bit more light there, and a counter I can spread out on.

I pull the papers we found in the prison camp from

my bag and smooth them out. There are five different documents, each about four pages long, and one that is much longer. I start with the shorter ones, flipping through them to see if there's any mention of the Phoenix or a reform school in Chicago.

There isn't.

I start on the longer one, but immediately shift gears. The document is titled "Root Operations," and it takes me only a minute of skimming to realize what I have. This is a list of Alliance cells, or "branches," as it calls them, around the United States.

It's single-spaced, printed two columns per page. It is fifty-three pages long.

I can't believe it. I *don't want to* believe it.

The city of Chicago alone takes up more than a page, with more than forty branches listed. They are listed by neighborhood — Bucktown Branch, Chinatown Branch, Humboldt Park Branch — but there are no addresses. The cells could be anywhere in those neighborhoods. Probably in plain sight.

And Maddie could be in any one of them.

Or could have been.

Troy's voice comes uninvited into my head again:

They shriek when you do it, like you're stealing their souls.

I shake it away and try to force my mind back to studying the Alliance papers.

How did you get out?

Shoot. It was the only way. They never even thought of it.

I try humming but nothing —

I won't let them take me back!

— drowns out his voice.

I put down the papers and fish in my pack for my compass and the map of Chicago and Environs I found in the bookstore in the abandoned mall. The map is old, from eight years ago, and half the markings on it are obsolete. There are no more amusement parks or post offices or general points of interest. But the major roads haven't changed, and they're the important part. They are what we need to avoid.

Out here where there aren't many people or many build-ings, not having our ID bracelets has been inconvenient but not impossible. But in Chicago it will be trickier. If we get spotted without our IDs, we'll be picked up and taken immediately to prison, and straightening that out would cost time we don't have.

Time Maddie doesn't have.

So we are going to have to be careful. Very careful.

My eyes slide down the map from central Chicago south to where my house is. It would be an additional three hours' walking to get there. Maybe once I've figured out where Maddie is —

I hear footsteps behind me and turn to see Alonso loping toward me. "I brought you breakfast," he says, and opens his palm to reveal a handful of chalky, anemic-looking, heart-shaped candies.

"Where did you find those?" I ask.

He points a thumb over his shoulder. "Valentine's Day section. They're called 'conversation hearts.' There are two dozen boxes still sealed up. Breakfast, lunch, and dinner. And wait until you try them. They look better than they taste."

"Didn't we decide this place closed five years ago? These are ancient."

"You mean aged." He flips through the candies in his hand, mumbling, "No, no. Nope."

I stand up to get a better look but he pulls his hand out of my line of vision. "What are you doing?"

"Composing. But I can't find — aha!" He puts four candies down on the counter next to me.

SUGAR. SWEET. SO FINE. CLOD9.

"It's a poem. See how the last part rhymes? I admit it's not my best work, but it's still early in the day."

He made me a poem. "'Clod nine'?" I read.

"I think that's supposed to be *cloud* nine. Typos seem to be an issue with these conversation hearts. The poem I did for Ryan was called 'he baby.'"

He made Ryan a poem, too. Probably he made one for everyone already and mine is last.

I put SUGAR in my mouth and bite down. "This tastes like chalk."

"Wait a second. That's when it opens up and — Yes, I can tell by the expression on your face. Chalk and bleach, right?"

"These are gross."

"These are the only food we have."

"I love them."

He tumbles a half dozen more hearts onto the counter next to me. "What's this?" he asks, picking up the Root Organization document.

"As far as I can tell, those are outposts of the Alliance in the US. I want to figure out where they are."

He flips through it. "This is crazy. There are hundreds." I watch his eyes move over the Chicago section, taking it in quickly. "I always knew Edgewater was a stronghold for evil," he says. "That's where my grandparents live. Albany Park Branch, Austin Branch, Beverly Branch. They're everywhere."

"But no addresses. And even if we get in, I keep thinking of what Troy said, about shooting being the only way to get out."

"First we have to find the places." He reads a little longer, then puts the list down. "Why is the Alliance obsessed with trees? Root, branches, like that?"

I shrug. "I have no idea."

Alonso leans over, running his finger down the list, saying the names aloud. "It's just so unbelievable. Coleman Branch. My aunt lives in Coleman. I wonder if she'd like to know she has an Alliance cell as a neighbor."

"Apparently we all do," I say.

"Douglass Branch. Pullman Branch. Lincoln Park Branch."

As he says each name, my eyes slide to the place on the map, and I feel another prick of homesickness. It is awful to think that our country is already so deeply infiltrated.

Alonso leans down on his forearms on the counter next to me. "It could be because I'm feeling poetic, but since the Alliance seems to like to use tree imagery, what if we're wrong about what Troy meant when he said, 'Shoot'? What if he meant a tree shoot?"

"You mean, like, he used a baby tree to escape?" I ask.

"Maybe. Or something about new growth, a new start, or —" He stands up fast, shaking his head. "Never mind; that's stupid," he says, shoving a handful of candies in his mouth at once.

78

I think back to that moment with Troy.

Look for the big lie —

What big lie?

No, I told you, *not lie —*

I'm staring at the map, like I'm seeing it for the first time. "It's not stupid," I say slowly. "It's — You figured it out."

Alonso begins coughing. White powder comes out of his mouth and gets on his hands. "What?"

"You're right." My brain is clicking through ideas.

Rosie and Louisa join us then, sucking on the candies. Louisa shifts her candy from one side of her mouth to the other. "What did he figure out?"

"Read me the last three again," I say to Alonso.

"Douglass. Pullman. Lincoln Park." He coughs again. "How did I figure it out? What do those have to do with saplings?"

"Nothing. It was what you said about us being wrong about the kind of shoot. When I asked how they escaped, Troy didn't say 'shoot,' S-H-O-O-T. He said 'chute,' C-H-U-T-E."

Nobody seems as excited about this as I am.

"Those locations you're reading, the Alliance branches? They're —" I spread my fingers over the locations on the map where there are little printed symbols corresponding with every one of the names he's said. I glance up at Alonso to make sure he's paying attention. But instead of the map, his eyes are on me, and they are big, and he has some candy powder on his cheek and he's looking at me like he really cares what I'm going to say and the words dry up in my throat.

"What are they?" Rosie demands. "Those places?"

"Libraries," I say, still looking at Alonso. "They're all libraries. After they were closed, the Alliance must have taken them over. Helen and Troy escaped through the book chute." I lift my hand off the map. "Um, thanks. That was a really smart idea."

Alonso does this closed-lip smile, then lowers his eyes half-shut, taps himself on the chest, and says, "Quietly brilliant." He turns to me. "But the real brilliant one is you. I just mumbled a little. You're the one who figured everything out."

"Yeah, Evelyn, that is pretty amazing," Rosie agrees.

My knees feel a little wobbly. This is Louisa's fault. If she hadn't said that she thought Alonso looked at me a certain way, then I wouldn't have wondered if he looked at me that way and I wouldn't have been looking at him looking or —

And anyway it's still not the way he looks at her when she says to him, "Of course we knew Evelyn was a genius but here we thought you were just a pretty face."

He laughs. Only a little. But more than he needs to, I think.

I don't have time for this, I remind myself. We need to find Maddie.

"All the libraries are marked on the map, and one of them must be Helen and Troy's school. Since they were taken away in a Rover the same way Maddie was, it could be where she's being held, too," I say.

Rosie scans the map, picking out the little book symbol that means library. "But there are dozens. How will we find the right one?"

"Before they all closed, the libraries had an internal

network to help you borrow material from different branches," I say. "If the Alliance has kept the same system, then if we can get into any library's computer system, we can access the whole network."

If they have . . . *then* we can. *But if not?* my brain asks. What *then?* A wave of panic washes over me.

"Hey, look what we found in the beach shack!" Ryan comes bounding over like a happy puppy. He is clutching what looks like a very old cell phone in each hand. Drew follows him at a slower pace.

"Have you been looting a museum?" Alonso asks. "Those things have to be ten years old. They're probably only 8G. They won't even connect to a network."

"Yeah, yeah, and we don't have a calling plan," Ryan says. "I know. But we were thinking we could —"

Louisa grabs them from Ryan. "Mod them into two-way communicators." She slides the backs of the phones off. "Oh, sure. Then we could break into teams and search for Maddie faster." Her eyes move to me. "We need some wire and batteries. Oh, and that staple remover from yesterday."

I'm not the only one gaping.

Louisa glances around as if perplexed why we're staring at her. "Maddie's dad trained in communication in the army. He taught Maddie and me how to do it when we were little. We were too small to have our own phones but he gave us some old ones and showed us how to make them talk to each other. It's easy."

"I have batteries," I finally say. "But I'm not sure about the wire."

"I bet there's some in that card we found last night," Alonso says. "The one that played a song."

I point behind me. "Right. I think that's still in aisle two, Grandparent Extortion."

Louisa takes the staple remover and my bag of batteries. "Good. I'll need another set of hands."

"I'll help you," Alonso offers. It doesn't bother me at all. In fact, I mostly feel sorry for him because his is a love that is doomed to fail, considering that Louisa blushes whenever she's near Ryan.

I think Alonso smiles at me as he goes by but I'm too busy looking at the map to notice.

Rosie bends over it next to me. She draws a curvy line down with her finger, using side roads to avoid the main highway, jiggling through the northern suburbs of Chicago. She says, "I think this is our best route. How about you, Evelyn?"

I slip my compass into my pocket. "Looks great," I tell her. It's really good having her back.

Once the cell phones are wired, we pack up, say good-bye to the Santa hamster and the leprechauns, and head back out.

We're two hours into our walk when we realize we've made a horrible mistake.

Chapter 6

The upside of using an old map is that it has the now-closed libraries on it. The downside is what it's missing.

According to the map, the area we're now walking through is filled with housing developments named things like Hobson Wood, Downer's Grove, and Century Dairylands, after the family farms that had once been there. But the buildings in those developments weren't made well enough to withstand the weather changes, so now they are all just uninhabitable rubble. Anything useful was taken away a long time ago, and there's no one here now.

I'm walking with Rosie and Louisa, with the boys behind us, but none of us is talking. Until now the only noise has been the crunching of our feet on the rocky path churned up by the bulldozers that moved some of the rubble away. But as we pass a peeling paint sign that says ELLSWORTH ACRES, pausing to check it against the map to make sure we're still going the right way, we begin to hear the faintest whistle of wind.

As we walk on, it gets louder. There is something about the sound it makes, like a witch singing a lullaby, that gives me goose bumps but makes me want to hear more at the same time. Maybe that's why, even when I feel the vibrations beneath my feet and my internal DANGER! alarm starts flashing, I don't say anything to Rosie and Louisa. By the time we see the first field of them, we've crossed the boundary and it's too late to turn back.

Breezers. I see them as we come over the crest of a hill. Hundreds of the squat mini-windmills that work well in flat areas, like the ones the government put up around the southern tip of Lake Michigan. Unlike the government breezer farms, though, these aren't set up in neat lines, but more like haphazard groves, each one ringed by a barbed wire–topped fence. That must be the source of the odd wind noise, I realize, the air moving through the barbed wire. But the arrangement still doesn't make sense. If they were all together, it woul —

Rosie's strong grip on my arm interrupts my thoughts and stops me in my tracks. She doesn't say anything, just points to the right of the breezers. My gaze follows her finger and I see a flash of light off a piece of metal. Then my eyes adjust and I register that it's not just a sheet of metal; it's a roof, one of dozens — no, of hundreds, no — as far as I can see, there's a motley quilt of roofs and tent peaks blanketing the land. My stomach lurches.

"Whoa. What the . . ." Alonso's voice trails off as he comes up beside me.

But I can't speak. It's Rosie who says, "It looks like we've wandered into the Settlement Lands."

None of us has ever been near the Settlement Lands, but all of us know what they are. They are the kind of place that you hear about only in the safety of your living room, in stories on the NewsServ, or in blogs.

At first those stories used words like "reunion," "families," and "new start." That was a few years ago, when the government set up tents and trailers to house the people from California and the South who came pouring into the middle of the country after they lost their homes to the rising waters. The tents were considered a temporary stop until the families got resettled. But since the War keeps getting worse, not better, and no new homes can be found for anyone, the temporary resettlement camps have become the permanent Settlement Lands. And now the stories about them involve words like "gangs," "murder," and "innocent bystander."

"Is there any way to avoid going through them?" Drew asks.

Rosie squints over the map and shakes her head.

"Can't we just go around?" Louisa asks.

I join Rosie at the map. Even though it's too old to have the Settlement Lands on it, it shows the developments whose names are most often associated with them, and they stretch in a band around northern Chicago. Trying to go around them will add four, if not more, hours to our trip. Four hours Maddie might not have.

"Our only option is to go through," I say.

"Maybe we should split up, so we don't draw as much attention to ourselves," Ryan says.

"If we do, I'm going with Rosie," Louisa announces.

"Me, too," I agree.

"Thanks, but we're not splitting up," Rosie tells us. "We stay together, keep moving, and don't bother anyone. Think of it like the first day at a new school — remain alert, but don't be obvious about it. We'll be fine."

I don't know if she believes it, but the way she says it makes me believe it. And everyone else, too, I think, since we all seem much less jumpy as we start walking again.

We pass near one of the groups of breezers. There's a hand-lettered sign that reads *Hello Daytime! Property KEEP OFF! Guard on duty at all times*, tied on to the fence but no evidence of anyone. The next group of breezers is larger, with a more official-looking sign saying *You Are Now Entering a Desert Fresh Facility* planted in front of a small shack.

"There's someone in there," I whisper to Rosie.

"Ignore him and keep walking," she says, and we do, although I notice us all pulling our sleeves down to cover where our missing ID bracelets should be.

Each of the stands of breezers has wires running from it. Although I doubt either the makers of Hello Daytime! vitamins or Desert Fresh Dry Shower Powder are in the business of generating energy, I'm pretty sure that's what is going on here. The wires crackle with electricity as we walk under them and into the settlement itself.

Like flipping a switch, the ground goes from rubble to some kind of street. As we keep walking in the direction my compass says is toward Chicago, the streets become more crowded, but apart from one or two small children, no one seems to be paying any attention to us.

Most people are going about their business the way they would anywhere, except instead of stores and houses made of bricks and stone, theirs are pieced together out of whatever is available: a car door, a balcony railing, a stop sign. To our left is a substantial structure with a bay window surrounded by bushels of hay. The door was once a table at a fast food restaurant with a yellow-and-red clown face on it.

We pass a bootleg software merchant who has decorated his booth with a fringe of finger-drives, a girl selling rice cakes off the back of a bike, a woman offering heavily patched T-shirts, a man with a greasy ponytail hawking Ozone Block SPF 350, which I know doesn't even exist. Everything is either a fake or secondhand.

Unlike in downtown Chicago, almost no one here is wearing a uniform of any kind. And unlike in downtown Chicago, every twenty or thirty feet, someone has painted three parallel black lines on the side of a building.

"What do those mean?" Louisa asks, pointing at the symbol.

"It's to show they support the Resistance," Rosie tells her. "The three stripes are the sign of the Hornet, the leader of the Resistance."

"The Hornet is a myth," Drew says.

Rosie shrugs. "Maybe. But if you talk to people in the Resistance, they believe in him."

"Have any of them actually *seen* him?" Drew asks.

Rosie stands up straighter and I get ready for her to give him a piece of her mind, but instead she says out of the corner of her mouth, "At the next alley, go left. No matter what, keep moving."

I look around and realize that as we've been talking, people have begun to disappear from the street. Not in a rush but still fast, melting into doorways and sliding into shadows until we are the only ones out.

And then it happens.

They appear almost out of nowhere. One second there's no one in the street in front of us; the next there are a dozen people blocking the way. They're all on bikes and scooters. They are about half girls and half boys. Several of them look really young, like ten or eleven, and none of them can be more than two years older than we are, but there's something serious and grown-up about them.

In the center of all of them is a bike that's got a buggy with a kind of canopy attached to it. The buggy is cobbled together from different car parts with the front made out of a piece of an old soda ad that says *Bring Dr. Yum Yum and have lots of Fun Fun.*

I do not think we are about to have a lot of fun fun, though.

The guy in the buggy seems to be the leader. He rises, puts one hand on either side of the canopy, and just stands there. It's hot but he's wearing long sleeves and a scarf and gloves. His face is visible, a few shades darker than mine, but his eyes are pale green, almost milky, from under the shadow of the canopy.

He's eyeing us like we're a new toy for him and his friends to play with. From the coolness of his stare and the fact that I now notice everyone in his gang is armed, we're not talking about a tea party.

We so don't have time for this.

He says, "This is Dr. Yum Yum gang territory. What brings you to our little paradise?"

There are a few chuckles from his posse.

"We came for the shopping," I say lightly.

Apparently he's the only one who is allowed to make jokes. He squints and leans forward. "You being funny?"

I shrug. "I was trying to, but I guess it didn't work.

What do you think I could have done to make it funnier? I'm always working to improve my act."

"Is she nuts?" he says, addressing the rest of our group.

"I'm afraid so," Drew says, stepping forward and resting his hand lightly on my shoulder. "She wandered away from our school and we were sent out to bring her back."

The guy in the buggy's expression changes and his strange pale eyes narrow. "You're scouts," he says, and spits afterward, like "scouts" is a bad word. "Filthy scouts."

"What's a scout?" I ask.

No one answers me, but the members of the Dr. Yum Yum gang seem to grow more alert. One girl on a scooter has pale skin and red hair and a set of spikes wrapped around her fingers. She keeps her eyes on us but says to the leader, "Want me to show them what we think of scouts, Bailey?"

The guy called Bailey scratches his chin and comes to a decision. "Round them up, Slam. Maybe we can trade them for something."

"No, no, no, this is a misunderstanding," I say. "We're not scouts; we don't even know what —"

"And shut that one up."

"Gladly," the red-haired girl, Slam, says. The littlest of the kids hops off the back of a bike and comes to steady the scooter as Slam steps from it.

I feel Rosie and Drew exchanging glances across me. We are outnumbered and outarmed. But we can't let ourselves be taken.

A loud whistle splits the air three times in succession.

"Mount up!" Bailey hollers. Slam jumps back onto her scooter, grabs the littlest kid around the waist, and all the riders take off in different directions, kicking up a cloud of dust.

"What just —?" Ryan starts to ask.

The dust settles, and, where the riders had been, there's now a Jeep parked sideways. The back fender of it says *Joey's Antidepression Drops. We care for you when you couldn't care less.* The front door reads MILITARY POLICE.

A soldier steps out of the Jeep. She's got a rifle across her chest and a helmet on, but beneath it her face is round and young. She's probably not even sixteen.

I can't decide if this is better or worse than the Dr. Yum Yum gang. On the one hand, there's only one of her.

"Hands up, wrists front," she calls, reaching for something on her belt.

On the other hand, the thing she's reaching for is an ID bracelet scanner.

"State your business here," she says.

I don't think my shopping line will go over this time but before I can think of anything else to say, Alonso steps forward. "We're on a school field trip," he says, sounding friendly. "We're studying the effects of migration on famili —"

"Get back there and put your wrists in the air," the soldier barks. She moves toward us with the ID scanner.

"But —"

"LINE UP AND SHUT UP!" she shouts. "Get those bracelets where I can see them."

Definitely worse. This is it. The end. Through her teeth, Rosie whispers, "Take the others and go. I'll create a —"

I see a flash of yellow out of the corner of my eye like a scarf. I hear a *whoooooooosh* and the area fills with smoke. The soldier starts to cough and I catch the sound of static and then her yelling into her walkie-talkie. "Incident in quadrant five, section eight. Requesting backup."

I can't see a thing but someone grabs my hand, and Rosie's voice in my ear says, "Run," and I do.

We run together, tripping, directly into the cloud of acrid smoke. I pull my T-shirt over my nose and mouth. My lungs are burning and my eyes are stinging and I can barely keep them open.

When the smoke begins to thin, I see that Louisa is holding Rosie's other hand. But Alonso, Drew, and Ryan have vanished.

Chapter 7

We can't stop," Rosie pants. "We have to keep moving."

"What was that?" Louisa coughs as we stagger on.

"Smoke bomb," I say. "We can't just abandon the others. We have to go back."

"No way," Rosie says, dragging me on.

From Louisa's pocket there's an odd squawking noise and Drew's voice crackling, "Team Beta, this is Team Alpha. Do you read?"

"It works," I say, amazed.

Rosie grabs it from Louisa. "We're Team Alpha; you're Team Beta," she says into the handset. "Where are you?"

"We'll talk about that alpha-beta thing later. We ran straight down. In front of us we see a big silver thing —"

"Us, too," Rosie cuts him off and we make for it as fast as we can.

"Who threw the smoke bomb?" Louisa is frowning. "Do you think it was that gang?"

"Doesn't matter. We lucked out," Rosie pants.

I agree, although that kind of luck makes me uneasy. "What do you think scouts are?" I ask.

"Something unpopular," Rosie says.

We meet up with the boys, but we don't stop running. In five minutes we cross a dry creek bed that seems to be the border of the Settlement Lands. We make it through but the landscape in front of us is not much more welcoming than what we've left.

We spend the next hour running through backyards that used to have sparkling blue pools and swing sets, jumping over squeaky hinged gates, and climbing fences. The windows of the houses all watch with blank, unoccupied disinterest. Where there are still doors, bright orange CLOSED BY ORDER OF THE RESOURCE ALLOCATION AND DEFENSE AGENCY labels flutter against them like pennants.

We're on the outskirts of Chicago but I've never been here. I was only eight when the first mandatory relocation plans went into effect, forcing residents on the edges of the city to move into central Chicago to save water and energy. I was not even ten when the relocation for security happened, so no one I knew ever lived out here.

The trees begin to rustle and the swings in a playground we run through start to sway with low squeaks from their rusty joints. Eddies of leaves swirl around our feet.

The wind is picking up. We're close enough to Chicago to be in the band of the mini-typhoon that's coming.

Louisa looks up at the lowering sky. "Are you sure we shouldn't just go to the police when we get to the city?"

"You saw what happened back there," I say. "Without ID bracelets, they'll arrest us instantly."

"Maybe it will work better if we go right to the station," Ryan suggests. "Then we could call our parents and they could explain it all —"

"Some of us could," Rosie cuts in.

"Plus, how seriously do you really think they'd take us? Six kids with no IDs who claim their friend was kidnapped by Alliance agents in the middle of the United States? I mean, that sounds nuts even to *me*." I tap myself on the chest. "And I was there."

Drew nods. "Evelyn is right. You can do what you want, but I'm not wasting time trying to explain things to the police and waiting for them to call my parents while Maddie is in the hands of her kidnappers. Finding Maddie is my number one priority."

"I agree," Rosie says. "But we have to be smart about it. We're too visible. We've got to take shelter. What we need to find is an abandoned building in the middle of the city with no nosy neighbors but solid construction and good drainage so it can withstand the storm."

"Oh, is that all? A completely habitable building that is uninhabited in the middle of the most overcrowded city in the US. No problem," Drew says.

"Yeah, while we're at it, I'd like to request a full-service all-you-can-eat buffet, a slick set of wheels, and some volumizing shampoo." Ryan pats his short hair. "I don't think my hair is doing all it could be for me."

Rosie looks at Louisa and me and rolls her eyes.

A few minutes later we pass a sign that reads, CHICAGO CITY LIMITS.

The five skyscrapers still standing in downtown Chicago loom in front of us, reflecting the gathering green-gray storm clouds like immense windows into another world. I know Rosie is right; going straight there without setting up camp first would mean taking unnecessary risks. Still, I find the closer we get, the more homesick I feel. In my pocket I wrap my hand around my compass.

All around us the empty houses show signs of having been struck by lightning storms. Those that are still standing are half-burned, dark husks with the occasional bathtub or dining table still inside. A piece of flowered wallpaper tumbles by us, carried on the wind.

The emptiness feels ominous to me. Or maybe it is just because the closer we get to learning the truth about where Maddie is, the more afraid I feel.

Louisa seems to get happier with every step. "We're finally here," she says, bouncing along next to me. "We could even have Maddie back by tonight, right? Tomorrow at the latest."

"Oh, completely," I say, trying to match her enthusiasm. And we could.

If she's alive.

But of course I don't say that out loud. How could I? What would it do besides upset them?

The first ribbons of lightning are beginning to mass on the horizon around the city, when it hits me that by not telling Louisa the whole story, by purposely shielding her from the truth, I'm doing what my parents do to me.

And that's when I realize: Maybe my parents don't do it to leave me out or exclude me. Maybe they say those things because they desperately want to believe them, too. They are protecting me and protecting themselves, trying to weave a cocoon of hope around all of us.

As the truth of this crashes over me, I miss my parents so much it makes me ache inside. I feel like for the first time I'm really understanding them. I want to apologize to them. I want to tell them I love them. I just want to hear their voices.

I look around at the desolate landscape we're running through, houses reduced to embers and rubble, and I wish I could close my eyes and be with them. Be safe.

How did I end up here? How did I end up so far from home?

I miss you, Mommy and Daddy.

I have an almost insurmountable urge to just stop. Sit down. Give up. What are we doing? How can we possibly think we can save Maddie? Six starving kids on the run with nothing but a compass, an old map, and a lame theory? There's no chance we can avoid being picked up by the authorities.

A ragged curtain of silver lightning appears in the sky to our left, followed by a plume of smoke as it sets a building on fire.

Assuming we're not incinerated first.

"No way," Louisa says. "Look."

My eyes follow her finger past three blackened carcasses of buildings to a squat, solid cement structure. The words LUXE LIFE CAR WASH are printed in faded paint on the side.

No neighbors. Built to withstand storms. Good drainage. And since there's not enough water to take showers, let alone wash cars, unlikely to be in use.

We run for it.

Inside, it's not exactly Cozy Corners.

The floor is blanketed with broken bottles and soda cans and pieces of debris. It turns out that those air freshener things that dangle from rearview mirrors don't smell better when they're old, moldy, and decaying.

But the building is fairly well boarded up so it's private, and, as the storm whips itself into a frenzy outside, it proves itself to be mostly leak free.

It's also only six blocks from the nearest library.

We spend the hour the storm lasts setting up camp. When the sky clears, it's almost three o'clock, at least according to the clock Rosie and Drew "borrowed" from a motel office when we first escaped from CMS. The six of us set out. We're on a double mission: to get into the library and to get food.

The car wash seems to mark the end of the relocation zone, and a block away from it, the houses show signs of being lived in. The streets are quiet now because most people keep factory hours, which run until five. The only person we come across is an elderly woman looking for her cat, but it is a good reminder that we need to start being more careful about where we go and when.

I check both my map and my compass when we get to 1150 West Fullerton Avenue to make sure we're in the right place. The building is made of brick and has a tower to one side, but there's nothing to show it was once a library. The sign outside says HELPING HANDS CHARITIES, REFUGEE RESOURCE CENTER.

The refugees must not get their help here, though, because the place is deserted. There's a single car in the parking lot with an ad for 2 GOOD 2 B TOFURKEY and the words MARTIN SECURITY on the side. There's no sign of anyone inside.

We split into two teams, Alpha team — Rosie, Ryan, and Louisa — going left, and Beta team — me, Alonso, and Drew — going right, both looking for a way into the building.

"All locked on our side," Rosie's voice says over the phone.

"Here, too," Alonso confirms. "But we might have something. Will keep you posted."

He, Drew, and I are standing at the bottom of a sloping driveway. There's a loading dock, a door, and two Dumpsters blocking the view from the street. Which means it's a good lock for us to try picking.

Drew kneels in front of the door with an unbent paper clip. "I used to pick the lock on my mom's office all the time," he says. "And it's a pretty serious lock." He turns to me. "Neither of you would happen to have a rubber band, would you?"

We've left our backpacks at the car wash, but I always carry a few essentials in the pockets of my pants. I fish out a rubber band and hand it to him. "Your mom works at home?" I ask.

"Kind of. It's more like we live at her office," he says, holding the paper clip between his teeth. "I think I've almost got —"

We hear the whine of brakes as a truck slows to turn into the driveway. The only possible cover is provided by the two Dumpsters, so we tuck ourselves behind them.

I hear a grinding noise from somewhere, and then the tiny beep of a truck going in reverse. From between the Dumpsters we watch a NutriCorp truck back toward the loading dock.

The driver honks his horn twice and the loading dock door rolls up.

"What's going on?" Rosie's voice squeaks through the phone, which Alonso quickly hides under his shirt.

But not quickly enough. The truck driver and the security guard have both turned to stare at the Dumpsters.

The security guard moves his hand toward the gun on his hip. "Hey, you there," he bellows in our direction, bobbing his head to get a better look. "Show yourself. *Now.*"

Chapter 8

Drew lurches out from behind the garbage can, staggers forward clutching his injured shoulder, and stumbles to the ground.

The deliveryman and the guard run toward him to help him. I'm just thinking we should have been more careful and let him heal longer, when he catches my eye from over their shoulders, and I realize he is causing a diversion.

Alonso gets it at the same time and without saying a word we climb the step to the loading dock, run through it, and enter the library.

It's dim and cool and quiet in here. Very, very quiet. We're on the main floor in what looks like it was once the entrance area. One side of it is stacked high with NutriCorp boxes.

Alonso points at the other side of the room where there's a curved desk with a sign reading CHECKOUT, and a computer. We start toward it but the voices of the deliveryman and the security guard start getting closer behind us. Alonso shakes his head and I agree. We need to move on.

We pass through a set of swinging double doors and find ourselves in a big room. Carefully stacked and color-coded NutriCorp boxes take up about half the space. The rest of it is a jumble of tables and chairs perched precariously on top of one another.

There are no computers.

Across the room there's a door ajar to what looks like an office. I point, Alonso nods, and we head toward it. A quick glance tells us there's no computer, and we're about to back out when there are voices and one of the double doors swings open.

We slip into the office and pull the door nearly shut, leaving us in the dark. Alonso peeks through the crack to monitor what's going on outside, and I scan the desk.

There's a phone and pieces of paper. There's also a little book of what look like weird crossword puzzles with hexagons instead of squares to write the letters in. Next to that is a photo in a frame. It shows a man holding a little girl with his arm wrapped around the waist of a woman. They are standing in front of the Field Museum before it was destroyed, smiling hugely at the camera. They look nothing like my parents, and the little girl looks nothing like me, but for some reason seeing that photo makes the ache of missing my parents come back.

I'm not even aware of what I'm doing. My hand reaches for the phone. Then my fingers are dialing the number of my house before my brain can kick in and tell me to stop.

It starts to ring. My hand is trembling.

I have no idea what I am planning to say, or how I plan to say it, since there are people outside the door. I just want to hear my parents' voices.

The phone keeps ringing. And ringing. And ringing.

No one answers, not Mr. Larson or Mr. Peña or even the voice mail. Which is weird. I picture the phone ringing, echoing through the entry hall and living room and dining room and den and kitchen. Up the dark wood staircase and along the corridor to my parents' room and my room and the guest room. Nobody. No one is home. No one knows I'm in trouble.

I know it's ridiculous but at this moment I feel more alone and lost than I have ever felt in my life. My fingers close around the compass in my pocket.

"They're gone." Alonso turns from the door. His eyes get huge when he sees me holding the phone. "What are you doing?" he demands.

I hang up. "It works," I say, not answering his question. Not looking at him. I don't want him to see the tears in my eyes. "I tried to call my parents but no one answered. Your turn." I push it toward him. I hope he didn't hear the crack in my voice.

He shakes his head. "We don't have time. Besides, my dad is impossible to reach. He's always traveling."

"What about your mom?"

I sense him stiffen. "She's dead." I look at him now but before I can say anything he puts his hand up. "It happened three years ago. I've dealt with it. No discussion needed."

I can't believe that is something you deal with in three years. Without meaning to, I blurt, "Is that why you don't like holidays?"

He jams his hands deep into his pockets, letting his hair fall over his eyes. "You're not really into the whole just-let-it-drop thing, are you?"

"I'm sorry. That was rude. Forget it."

He nods. "I spotted a sign pointing downstairs for the circulation office. You mentioned the library network was to help move books from one place to another so maybe there's a computer there."

"Great idea," I say, probably too brightly because I'm trying to make up for asking him too much.

We leave the office and go down a set of narrow marble stairs. At the bottom there's a corridor with cube offices on both sides. They're all empty, and I think that this must be what it looks like for the mice they use in those navigating-a-maze-for-a-piece-of-cheese experiments.

Along the far wall there are offices, most of them empty. But the one with CIRCULATION on the door has the blinds up and we see a computer on the desk.

"I think that computer was born before I was," Alonso says, and I agree. It has a flat screen and a long plastic keyboard with individual keys instead of a tablet, and each piece is attached to the others with cables.

The desk is cluttered with objects, a little stone frog, a cup with pens — PENS! — in it, typed cards, a rubber ball, a six-sided cube with different-colored blocks. It must be a woman's office because there's also a compact of eye shadow and a sample of perfume.

"Hello, old friend," Alonso says, hefting a big book off the floor. He blows dust off the cover. "I have one just like this at home."

"A dictionary?" I slide into the seat in front of the computer. "Why?"

"It was my grandfather's," he says with a shrug. "I used to read it before I went to bed."

I look up at him to see if he's kidding, but he's busy paging through the book. "That's — that's really cool," I tell him.

He closes the dictionary abruptly, like maybe he's embarrassed. "Yeah, I really only looked at the pictures."

114

He puts the dictionary down and points to an oval thing about the size of my palm with a blinking light on it. "What do you think that does?"

"I've seen them in movies. Before touch screens and navpads, they used them. I think it's called a 'mouse.'"

He glances around the office. "I feel like we're in the Stone Age. You know how to drive this thing?"

"I think so," I say, pulling the keyboard toward me. I hit some of the keys experimentally. Each one makes a clicking noise that sounds loud in the silence of the building, but it works, and the screen comes to life. A box pops up asking me for a password.

Hurdle one.

"Can you get through the encryption?" Alonso asks. He's playing with things on the desk, picking them up and putting them down.

"I can try but it might take a little while."

I bypass the password screen by opening up a programming window. Whatever this operating system is, it's old and slow.

Alonso leans over to pick up the pencil cup and looks underneath it.

The programming window closes abruptly with a beep and the password box comes back up.

My heart is going unusually fast. It's true that back home, sometimes (okay, daily) I'd go on my computer to do research that involved having to hack around the security protocols and firewalls that my parents have installed to keep me from doing that research. But I've never (successfully) hacked into anyone else's server, not with a friend's life on the line, and not one running ancient software.

I try all the basic passwords, consecutive numbers, consecutive letters of the alphabet, things my parents use.

A second after I type each one, the computer beeps.
UNSUCCESSFUL ATTEMPT. PLEASE ENTER PASSWORD.

Alonso opens, then closes, the eye shadow compact. He slides open the drawer next to me.

"Can you stop, please?" I say. "That's really distracting."

I start trying months of the year. Eight clicks for "December." *Beep.* Seven clicks for "January." *Beep.* I swear the key clicks are getting louder. Five clicks for "March." *Beep.*

Alonso closes the drawer and stands behind me with his arms crossed, which is not less distracting. "Try 'clover,'" he says.

Six clicks. *Beep.*

He leans down and stares at the keyboard. "Sorry. Clover with a zero instead of the letter *O*."

I do it.

We're in.

"How did you do that?"

He slides open the drawer and points where 'cl0ver' is taped to the front of it. "You can't be expected to find all the answers on your own."

"I shouldn't have yelled at you," I say.

He points to the screen. "Don't worry about it. Go."

The homesite that comes up is for Helping Hands Charities, an organization whose mission is "to improve the lot of the poor and suffering in all lands, through equitable resource allocation and refugee outreach for a better tomorrow."

"That doesn't sound evil," Alonso says. "Although if you squint, the two entwined hands of their logo look a lot like the Alliance symbol."

He's right. I type Maddie's name into the Site Search field but that brings no results.

I click on the different menu items — Food, Shelter, Recycling, Rebuilding, Become a Volunteer — but each one just brings up pages for their different "charitable undertakings."

"This is sick," Alonso says, watching the praise from different politicians scroll past in the Press section. I agree, but I'm too tense to talk. As far as I can see, Helping Hands is a completely legitimate organization. Could I have been wrong? Could the libraries not be Alliance havens?

There has to be a way to get past this portal and into the actual nuts and bolts of the network. I click on every possible menu item, looking for a hidden doorway. Every page takes seconds to load. Seconds during which someone could figure out we're here. Seconds of Maddie's life.

Nothing nothing nothing. *Clickclickclick*. Even the keyboard feels slow.

My stomach is in knots and I feel tears pricking the edges of my eyes.

There are footsteps above us.

"They're way up there, we're way down here. Don't worry," Alonso says soothingly. "Wait a second — go back."

I click the "back" button on the browser to a Recycling Resource Management page.

"There," he says, pointing to a photo along the side. It shows a group of kids in front of a sign with a bird rising from what look like red ribbons.

"Didn't that Troy guy mention the phoenix? Well, that's a phoenix," Alonso explains. "It's a mythical bird that dies and then rises renewed from its own ashes." He fiddles with the cuff of his sweatshirt like he feels self-conscious for knowing that. "There's, um, a picture of it in the dictionary."

"Of course." I click on the photo. Another page comes up, this time about the Phoenix Center Program for

Children in Trouble — "Because the Children are Our Best Resource."

Phoenix, what Troy was so afraid of being returned to, is a *school*, not a person.

Possibly the school where Maddie is being held.

I click quickly through all the photos, but they are all taken indoors. There's no way to tell where Phoenix Center is, and none of the information has an address.

The clock ticks on. I curl my hands into fists and bring one down on the keyboard.

The screen vanishes. It's replaced by a programming box with a flashing cursor.

"What the —"

"We're in," I tell Alonso.

Somehow we've gotten behind the Web site into the network. I stop being aware of time or where I am as I slip into the main directory of the Alliance in Chicago. There are files on operations and files on supplies and files on weapons and engagement reports and reams and reams of information.

Finding Maddie's name in this is going to be like finding a needle in a thousand haystacks.

"This is incredible," I breathe aloud.

"Can you find Maddie?"

"I'm trying."

The clicking of the keyboard sounds like a sudden rainstorm as my fingers move faster than they ever have. I write a search bot to find any mentions of M. Frye.

I get more than a thousand hits.

I don't have time for that. I start over with Madeleine Frye.

And there it is.

Madeleine Frye. Phoenix Program HW Branch. Status: AL5. Transfer to Bright Spa in 23:25:11. As I watch, the transport clock ticks down the seconds and I realize she's going to be moved in less than twenty-four hours.

"She's alive. She's alive and we found her." I can't keep the tears out of my eyes.

Chapter 9

W hat's wrong?" Alonso asks, looking really alarmed. I guess crying girls are a little scary. "Did you lose your compass?"

That makes me smile for a second. "I — I thought she was dead," I say. "Maddie. I couldn't figure out why they kidnapped her except to lure us into a trap or as a lesson to our parents, and I thought —"

"That's why you were so tense the other night when Louisa started asking why they'd kidnapped Maddie," he says.

That surprises me. "You noticed?"

"You hid it well, but I — I felt like there was something going on." He nods. "Why didn't you say something?"

"Because I didn't know if I was right or it was just another of my crazy theories. And because it would have upset everyone for no reason."

"You could have told me."

I am looking up at him and I have that strange feeling again.

"You can always tell me your crazy theories," he goes on. "It can still be a secret if you share it with one other person. And it will make you feel better."

"I guess."

"And maybe they'll have other ideas. Like remember how Louisa said Maddie's dad was a communications expert? That could be why she was taken."

"You're right," I say.

I don't realize I'm staring at him until he makes a point of gesturing at the screen. "But now that we found Maddie, we should probably go. Especially since she's going to be moved around this time tomorrow."

It's true. But I just want to check one more thing. I quickly write a bot to scan for Wren Chavez.

Nothing comes up.

But the amount of information on here is incredible. If only there were some way to insert a wormhole so the Resistance or the army could get access, I think, typing furiously.

I'm in kind of a daze so I only half pay attention when Alonso says, "Can you erase the evidence of your searches?"

"Mm-hmm," I answer.

"Evelyn," he says, and I look up from what I'm typing. "We have to move."

"I just need a few more minutes. You don't understand. This could change the War. If I —"

"We don't have time for that. We can't risk leaving any traces of what you're doing. If they discover we were looking for Maddie, she's as good as moved before we get there."

"Sure, you bet," I say, still typing. "Just one more thing."

There are more footsteps upstairs.

"We have to leave," Alonso says with new urgency that jolts me out of what I am doing.

I stop searching and look for an "erase history" tab but of course that would be too easy, so I go into the main directory and start deleting logs.

This computer moves at the pace of a glacier.

"Come on — we have to go," Alonso urges. He's half-in and half-out of the door, squeezing the rubber ball that had been on the desk.

"If there is a picture in the dictionary of 'slow,' I bet it would be this computer," I say. "I'm not quite finished."

"That doesn't matter. Listen," he says. "What do you hear?"

"Noth —" That's when I get it. All the traffic noise from outside has stopped.

He nods. "There must be police or something out there. I think they must have —"

The phone bleats to life and Rosie's voice crackles, "GET OUT NOW!"

"This way," Alonso says, grabbing my hand and pull-ing me down the hall toward a door marked EMERGENCY EXIT. He opens it, but right before we step in we hear footsteps coming in our direction from above.

A woman's voice echoing from a walkie-talkie squawks, "Fan out and check every floor."

Alonso puts his finger to his lips, pulls the rubber ball out of his pocket, and sends it bouncing down the stairs.

He pulls the emergency exit door almost closed and we huddle around the corner, close enough to hear a voice on the stairs say, "I've got them headed down from B to the subbasement. Yellowsquad, they are headed your way. I repeat: They are headed to SB level; all squads, all colors GO."

We wait as three sets of heavy boots pound down the stairs. My heart is flying. When they're past, we push through the EXIT door and climb the other direction. We pass the door marked GROUND LEVEL, assuming there will be guards there. When we get to two, we pause, but right before I push open the door we hear the faint sounds of a walkie-talkie. Alonso points up and I nod.

At the third floor Alonso pauses and pulls the eye shadow compact that had been on the desk downstairs out of his pocket. I stare at him, my eyes saying, *Are you sure this is the time to experiment with makeup?* and his saying back, *Watch and learn.* He eases the door open an inch and uses the mirror to see if there's anyone there, then opens it all the way, motioning me to follow.

This floor seems completely abandoned. The light through the windows gives a gauzy, surreal quality to the row after row of shelves lined . . . with books. Hundreds of them.

My breath is caught in my chest and the hair stands up on my arms. It is — this place is so beautiful.

I've never seen anything like this. I let my fingers run lightly over the spines of the books, tracing lines in the dust, astonished by the sheer weight of them. I feel like I've entered a magical, enchanted forest where anything is possible. I almost wouldn't be surprised to see a unicorn or a gossamer-winged fairy emerge from between the books.

I *am* surprised when we turn a corner and almost trip over a security guard with his feet up on a desk, sleeping. We back into the nearest aisle and move quickly in the direction we came from, but before we get far Rosie's voice says, "Do you read?"

Alonso jerks the volume off but not before the guard wakes up. I hear the sound of a chair being pushed back and the guard getting to his feet. "Hey," he calls after us. "What's the big idea?"

"Follow me," Alonso whispers, weaving in and out of the bookshelves. We dead-end at a wall, and turn left. Another dead end. The guard is slow but he's figured out where we're heading and we hear his footsteps getting louder.

"Hey, this is Harvey on three," we hear him panting into his walkie-talkie. "I think I got your intruders cornered up here."

He's right. It's another dead end, but at least this time there's a door. The top half is a glass panel with MEN written on it, glowing gently. Alonso points at the door and I follow him through it, turning the lock with shaking fingers as it closes behind us.

I've never been in a men's room before. There are two stalls with toilets, two sinks, two things that look like long sinks but I am pretty sure are for something else, and a tall window.

There's no place to hide.

The guard's footsteps are coming up fast. The handle of the door turns and he tugs on it, making the glass panel rattle back and forth.

"I've got them trapped in the men's room," we hear him say.

"What now?" I whisper to Alonso, but he's not next to me. I turn and see he's at the window, fiddling with the latch at the top. He springs it and pushes the window open, letting in a blast of cool air. I move closer as he climbs up into the frame. He glances down at me and gestures for me to join him.

From the window I can see the tops of other buildings. At our eye level. We're high above the ground.

I swallow. "You go. I'll —" There's a jingling outside the door, the sound of the security guard trying different keys in the lock. "I'll keep the guard off."

"Come on," Alonso whispers insistently.

I shake my head. "I can't. I — I'm afraid of heights."

The expression in his eyes instantly softens. He extends his arm. "Take my hand." I hesitate. "I promise it will be okay."

"It might not be. We could fall and fracture one of our wrists. Or break a leg. Or a rib. Or if we jump wrong, we could crack our heads open. I can think of a thousand things that could go wrong."

"You're right." Alonso nods thoughtfully, as though I am not acting like a complete nutcase. "But the only thing that is guaranteed to happen is if we don't jump, we'll get caught." Keys jingle. The door handle jiggles, harder this time. Alonso glances at it, then back at me. He says, "Trust me."

I reach out and put my palm against his. He laces his fingers through mine and pulls me up next to him.

I'm glad it's getting dark because I am pretty sure I'm blushing. I feel like someone has pinned my eyes open and I can't blink.

"Don't look down," he whispers into my ear, and now I know I'm blushing. "We'll jump on the count of three."

Another key is slotted into the lock.

"I can't," I say.

He squeezes my hand. "Look at me." I drag my eyes from the roofs of the other buildings, some of them *below* us. His eyes are brown pools of comfort. "Evelyn Posner can do anything. Now, let's count together. One."

"One," I whisper. My tongue feels too big for my mouth. "What direction do you think we're facing?"

He says, "Two."

"Two," I say.

The lock clicks open behind us.

"Thr —"

"Gotcha!" the security guard yells, wrapping his fingers around Alonso's ankle.

Chapter 10

Alonso says, "I think we're going due south," gives the security guard a hard kick, and then we're falling through space down three stories.

On the theory that if I keep my eyes closed, my life can't pass in front of them and therefore I can't die, they're shut when we land.

So it takes me a moment to realize that not only are we not dead, but also I'm not hurt. The ground beneath my hand is uneven and springy. Opening my eyes, I see we've landed on the surprisingly cushy fake grass border that runs along the edge of the library.

I will never say another mean thing about PlastiGrass for the rest of my life.

I can't hear anything because my heart is pounding so loudly in my ears, but Alonso's mouth is moving and he's pointing up, and when I follow the direction of his finger I see the security guard leaning out the window, fiddling with his walkie-talkie.

I look down and see that we are still holding hands. Alonso squeezes mine and nods, and I feel happy and like I want to cry at the same time.

We get up and I take a second to orient myself. We've come out on one side of the building, near the back. The loading dock where we are supposed to meet Rosie, Ryan, and Louisa is to our right. Two steps take us to the corner, but as we round it, we stop. Instead of Rosie and Ryan and Louisa, there are half a dozen police cars.

"Backup plan," I say. Alonso nods. We've taken two steps in the other direction when I feel Alonso jerk his hand out of mine.

"I'm sorry." I gulp, embarrassed. I must have been squeezing it. But when I turn around he's leaning over, gripping his knee.

"No, it wasn't you." His face is a twisted grimace. "I bashed my knee when I was trying to get rid of the security guard."

"Can you walk?"

"Oh yeah," he says, standing up. "I'm sure it's not —" He takes a step and stumbles, plunging face-first back into the fake grass.

I hear walkie-talkie static and then footsteps from the direction of the police cars. We have to get out of here.

"Here, lean on me," I say, draping his arm over my shoulder.

The guard has disappeared from the window but I still think we should take evasive measures. So we cross the street and crouch behind some bushes along the side of a house. From inside we can hear the low buzz of a NewsServ but not what it's saying.

"I hope they didn't get Rosie, Ryan, and Louisa," Alonso whispers.

"I don't see them in the cars. And since they had time to warn us, I'm guessing they got —" I cut myself off as the crunch of footsteps approaches the bushes where we are hiding. They stop right in front of us.

I hold my breath.

A hand reaches through the bushes and taps me on the head, and a voice says, "You're it!"

But not a police officer's voice. A little girl's voice.

Alonso and I exchange glances.

"I found you," the girl says. She leans over the bush. She looks to be maybe five. Her hair is in pigtails and one of the bows has come untied. She seems cute and sweet. She must live in the house we're crouching beside. "You come out," she says. "It's my turn to hide."

Alonso says, "We can't. We're playing with those men over there. See them?"

She glances toward the police, then back at us, and nods.

"If we come out now, they'll win," Alonso elaborates. "You don't want the grown-ups to win, do you?"

She thinks about this. Then her eyes narrow and suddenly she doesn't look so sweet. She says, "What'll you give me not to tell on you?"

Alonso grimaces as he shifts to reach into his pocket, pulling out the eye shadow compact. "This," he says. "It's a pretty color."

The girl sneers at him. "No way. I want that." She points at me. "What is it?"

"That" turns out to be my compass, which out of nervous habit I've taken from my pocket and am holding in my hand.

"You don't want that," Alonso says dismissively. "It doesn't even tell the time."

She holds out her hand. "Give it to me or I go tell one of those men where to find you."

Alonso looks at me and his expression says, *You don't have to give in to this little troll tyrant.* Maybe because of that, or maybe because the little girl then says, "There's a big fat one coming this way right now," I reach up and hand her the compass.

She looks at it, sticks out her tongue at us, and skips away.

"What are they teaching the children these days?" Alonso asks rhetorically. He has the compact open and is using the mirror to watch her through the bushes.

"What's she doing?"

"Well, she went straight up to one of the cops and started talking to him. He looks interested. Now she's nodding. Now she's pointing —"

We're both poised to run.

"— away from us. And they seem to be listening."

The next moment I hear doors slamming and engines starting, and, like a flock of birds taking off in unison, the police speed away in a flurry of wailing sirens.

When the cries of the sirens have diminished to a distant moan, I slide out of our hiding place. As we stand up, I realize I've been holding my breath.

Alonso leans heavily against the bushes. The slightly green color of his skin and the tightness of his jaw make it clear that he's in a lot of pain.

I hold out my arm. "Lean on me," I say, and he shakes his head. "Seriously, don't be stupid."

He slings his arm over my shoulder and we start walking back to the car wash.

"I'm sorry about your compass," he says.

"Don't worry. I'm sure I can get another one," I say as casually as I can, even though the thought of being without it is causing me a little panic.

We have only six blocks to go but it feels farther. Partially, I suspect, because the whole jumping-to-your-(maybe)-death-and-being-on-the-run-from-the-police thing has left my legs kind of wobbly. It's just past factory closing time, so there are more people on the street than there were when we walked over. At first that worries me, but no one seems to pay us any special attention, and I realize a guy walking with his arm across a girl's shoulders probably just looks like two teenagers out on a date.

Which makes my legs feel even more unsteady. I have a sudden strong urge to check our direction on my compass, and I'm already reaching for it before I remember it's not there.

At the next intersection we have to stop and wait for the light. I look up at Alonso to see how he's doing.

He smiles at me. "You were really brave back there," he says.

I get that weird feeling in my stomach again. "We wouldn't have had to be brave if I'd listened to you and left when you first said we should. You got hurt because of me."

"I got hurt because of that security guard. And not badly hurt. Although I'm really looking forward to seeing Louisa."

My stomach bounces like that rubber ball.

"I want to tell you something," he says.

"You don't have to," I assure him quickly, wondering how long until the light changes. "I know."

"You do?" He looks genuinely surprised.

"Yes." He opens his mouth but I rush on. "I know there's someone — special to you," I say. "I figured it out at the party store."

His mouth makes an *O* shape. He nods, like he's remembering something. "Right. What you said before about the holidays."

"No, not then, after."

"After? How?"

"You weren't exactly subtle. I have eyes." And ears, I

want to add, remembering how he cracked up at Louisa's joke. "The way you always try to make her laugh and help her out."

I'm avoiding his eyes but I can tell he's staring at me. "I don't think we're talking about the same thing."

I can tell he's uncomfortable so I try to think of the most tactful way to put it. "Yes, we are. We're talking about how there's someone you like. But . . . I'm afraid she doesn't have the same feelings for you."

I sense him try to stand up straighter next to me, like he's tense. I feel horrible. "She doesn't?"

"No. I'm sorry. I just — I don't want you to get hurt."

"Oh. Okay," he says, looking straight ahead. "Thanks for the heads-up. But —"

He sounds so sad. "I think Louisa is wrong," I say impulsively to cheer him up. "Personally I think you're great and you used to read the dictionary, which I think is one of the cutest things ever, but —" I stop myself when I realize what I've said.

At this moment I wouldn't mind if some police came and took me away. The light changes and we start walking and I hope that will be the end of it. But of course, no.

I feel his eyes on me. "*Louisa?*" he repeats.

"Don't deny it. Don't say anything. I just thought I should tell you," I stammer, concentrating on weaving through the other pedestrians. I feel totally lost and I hate that feeling. I wish life came with an emotional compass.

"That's not actually what I was going to tell you."

I don't want to look at him but I can't help it.

"What I was going to tell you is that you were right. In the office with the phone? What you said about me not liking holidays because of my mom dying. My father travels all the time, and so without my mom, holidays just feel empty." He exhales. "It's kind of hard to talk about so mostly I don't tell people."

My chest feels tight. "Thanks for telling me."

"After I said all that stuff about how you don't have to keep secrets alone, I figured I owed you. And it turns out I was right. I do feel better."

"Just another sign of your quiet brilliance," I joke as we cross from the sidewalk onto the pavement of the car wash.

He laughs. "Right." He pushes his hair off his fore-head. "And about that other thing —" he starts to say, but before he gets any further Rosie is running across the pavement toward us.

Her eyes are huge. "How did you get here?" she demands, turning to walk with us to the door.

"We hobbled." Alonso points at his knee. "War injury." We go inside and he lifts his arm from my shoulder.

Rosie is still looking strange. "But the police had the place covered."

"They went down; we went up," Alonso says. He turns to me. "Can we finish what we were discussing later?"

"Sure, yeah," I say, meaning "No, never, are you insane?"

"Why didn't you answer on the phone?" Rosie demands.

"We had to turn it off," I tell her. "We got up to the third floor and there was a guard there sleeping and —" My voice trails off. Louisa, Ryan, and Drew have circled around and I realize they're all looking at us like we've risen from the dead. Can they tell that we were holding hands?

"What's going on?" I ask.

Drew says, "When the police came, over the walkie-talkie, they didn't just say there was an intruder. They said the intruder was Evelyn Posner."

I feel the blood drain from my face. "The police knew my name?" I say. "But — but how?"

"Someone must be watching us," Rosie says. "Or —" She looks around, and I know what's coming, and I can also tell she's hating saying it. "Or one of us is a traitor."

I look from one to another of my friends' faces and I can't believe it.

I think about joking with Louisa in the drive-in about fixin's. About how Rosie sacrificed a chance to find Wren to save us. About what Alonso just confided in me about missing his mom. They're more than friends to me. They've become my new family.

Family.

That's when I realize that Rosie is right. One of us *is* a traitor.

And I know who.

Chapter 11

I take a step away from the others.

"It's me," I say.

They stare at me and I rush on. "I didn't mean to be a traitor, but it's my fault the police knew I was there. I — there was a phone at the library and we were hiding and it didn't seem like anything bad could happen, and I — I called home. They must have traced the call."

"If they're tracing all the calls out of the library, they must have your name on some kind of watch list," Alonso says.

"Either that or the Alliance is tracing all calls to our parents," Drew counters.

Neither of those is a very happy thought. Louisa's mouth is moving but no sounds are coming out. Finally she says, "But — but that means we can't go home. People from the Alliance could be waiting for us *at our homes*."

"It might not be the Alliance," I say, even though I don't believe it. "Maybe it's a team sent out to find — what?" I break off.

Rosie is standing in front of me with her hands over her mouth shaking her head. "Oh no," she says. "It is the Alliance. It has to be."

"What is it?"

I move toward her, and it's only because I am so close that I can hear it when she whispers, "Maddie. That's how they found her. It *is* my fault."

Not this again.

Rosie drops her hands but her face is bleak. She looks at Drew and says, "You know I'm right."

His expression goes from confused to understanding. He puts up a hand. "Wait a second, Rosie. It's not that simple."

"What are you two talking about?" I demand.

"The night before Maddie was taken, when Drew and I were at the gas station looking around, there was a pay phone," Rosie says. "And I tried to call my parents. No one answered, so I didn't think anything of it. But now . . ." Her voice trails off.

"Maddie wasn't taken until the next day," Ryan points out.

Drew puts in, "And that truck driver Gladys Cato saw us. It's a lot more likely that they found her that way."

"I guess," Rosie says, completely unconvinced. "But —"

"It really doesn't matter," I rush to say. "What matters is that we know we can't make any kind of contact with our parents." I push aside the slight pang I feel. There's too much at stake for homesickness. "At least not until Maddie is safe."

Alonso gives one of his mischievous smiles and stands with his hands in his pockets. "But that shouldn't be too long now. Because we figured out where she is."

Rosie rallies. "What? Why didn't you say that before?"

"You didn't give us a chance," I say. "She's someplace called the HW Branch. I'm pretty sure I remember seeing it on the map."

"This calls for a celebration," Ryan announces. "Anyone care for some tofu chili in hot, medium, or mild?"

"Yeah, I'd love some of all three. And if you have crispycakes and fizzy lemon soda, I'd take those as well," Alonso says, playing along.

"Okay, break it out." Ryan rubs his hands together. "What food did you bring back from the library? I'm starving."

The others all glance from him to us expectantly.

Alonso and I look at each other with shock. We didn't just not *bring* any food.

"We forgot to even look for food," I gasp. "And it's my fault because I spent so long —"

"No, it's my fault because while you were on the computer, I could —"

"— even though you kept saying we should —"

"— or at least been looking around instead of —"

"That's really too bad," Ryan breaks in, and he's so angry that his voice is quivering. I've never seen anything like the expression on his face.

"Yeah," Louisa snarls. Her eyes are bright with fury. "I guess we'll just have to make do with this." She bends and whisks away a tarp I hadn't even noticed on the ground.

Beneath it are cans of tofu chili and bottles of soda and bags of pretzels and soychips and apple snips and crackers and I even make out the bright orange top of a can of Cheezy-Wizard and something in a silver wrapper that looks like a dessert. I feel like I should rub my eyes to make sure I'm not dreaming.

"What? How?" I try to ask but my questions are drowned out by Rosie, Drew, Ryan, and Louisa laughing so hard they almost choke themselves.

"Evelyn's face when you asked about the food —" Rosie says, sputtering. "It was —"

Ryan gasps for air. "I know. And Alonso's eyes. They looked like they were going to pop out!" He clutches his stomach.

Louisa has tears running down her face. "And when they were each" — *hiccup* — "trying to take the" — *hiccup* — "blame —"

Rosie wipes her nose on her sleeve and stands, giggling and shaking her head. "Yeah, because hacking the computer, finding Maddie, and escaping from a full police cordon wasn't enough. Ever the overachiever." For some reason having her say that makes my cheeks feel warm.

Drew, who has gone to stand next to the stash of food, clears his throat. When we turn to face him, he points like a tour guide showing off a city. "The fizzy lemon soda is over there, but I'm afraid there aren't any crispycakes because those aren't a NutriCorp product. There are crispy*snacks*, though, and butterscotch, choco-late, and berry bars."

"It's beautiful," Alonso breathes, and I have to agree with him.

Rosie takes a long deep breath and gets really serious. "Do you two have any idea how scared we were?" she asks. "When we heard them saying Evelyn's name and then you just disappeared?"

I shake my head.

"Don't do that again," Rosie says.

Alonso gestures at the stash of food. "You must have been scared enough for Ryan to lose his appetite, or none of this would still be here."

"Well, I did try the soychili," Ryan admits.

We *all* start laughing then and I realize this isn't regular laughter. This is a kind of laughter you can have only when you've been through some really scary stuff together.

And have some really scary stuff still to face.

Ryan's still defending himself, saying, "Really it was just to make sure the food wasn't drugged like the stuff we found in that prison camp," as we each take our favorite things from the unbelievable selection. For the first time in days, there's more than just nuts and berries. And more than just enough. There's no reason to ration.

Rosie, Louisa, and I sit off to the side by ourselves while the boys stay within easy reaching distance of all the food. As we eat, Louisa and Rosie tell me about how they took advantage of Drew distracting the security guard outside the library to "liberate" the food from the back of the truck. Then Drew made a miraculous recovery and ran off to join them. I tell them about Phoenix and escaping from the guard.

"I can't believe you had to go into a boys' bathroom," Rosie says. She looks at Louisa. "Do you think she needs a special shot after that to make sure she doesn't have a disease, doc?"

Louisa laughs. "I'll keep an eye on her." Then she gets serious. She says, "Maddie is lucky to have friends like you. And so am I." And reaches out to gather Rosie and me into a hug.

"Me, too," I agree.

"Yeah, you guys are okay," Rosie says casually. But she hugs us the hardest of all.

Alonso must have told the boys about what we found because when we move back toward the food, Drew is saying, "So Phoenix isn't a person; it's a school. And you're sure that's where Maddie is?"

Alonso's lying on his stomach, propped on his elbows. "Yep, but only until tomorrow night. So we'll have to get her during the day." He looks at me as I sit down cross-legged. "Right?"

151

I nod.

"And we better not mess up," Rosie says. She and Louisa are sitting back to back. "Or we'll have to find this Bright Spa place. And it doesn't sound like a library."

Louisa twists her neck to glance at the clock. "Are you sure it's too late to try tonight?"

I know exactly how she feels. But I've also glanced at the map and learned that the HW Branch is the Harold Washington Library, and it's more than an hour's walk away. "It's after six. We'd be out way after curfew."

Ryan is lying on his side with his head propped on his palm. He opens his mouth and Rosie says, "Let me guess — you're going to suggest we hot-wire a car."

"No," he says in a way that makes it clear that he totally was. "I, was, um —"

"What about a bus?" Louisa offers. "We saw one when we were at the other library, so they must run out here. I still have my bus pass and it should have enough credit on it for everyone."

Alonso turns sideways to pull a pamphlet out of the pocket of his cargo pants. Clearing his throat, he reads,

"The Harold Washington Library is served by several of the city's main bus lines." He holds up what he's reading from. "At least according to the 2012 Guide to the Chicago Library System I picked up today."

"That was when it *was* a library," I point out.

"It's still a good idea." Drew moves his pack so he can lean on it like a pillow. "Any bus that goes south will at least get us closer and mean less time on the street."

"Not tonight." Rosie shakes her head definitively. "We have no idea what this place is like. We're going to need time to look around. Does the pamphlet say anything that could be helpful?"

Alonso skims along. "Four large winged beasts on the corner . . . glass-roofed atrium on the top available for parties . . . state-of-the-art children's library . . . huh."

"What?" Ryan asks.

"The good news is, there's probably a lot of places to hide if blending in doesn't work," Alonso tells us. "The bad news is that's because when it was built, the Harold Washington Library was the largest public building in America. Nine huge floors and four subbasements."

Drew's taken off his glasses and is staring at the roof of the car wash. "That's a lot of real estate to find one person without being spotted."

Even splitting into two teams, it could take us... more time than we have. As the stark truth of his words sinks in, silence falls like a heavy blanket over us.

Until Rosie sits up, sending Louisa tipping sideways. "But don't you see?" Rosie says, looking around at all of us with bright, excited eyes. "Being spotted is the one thing we don't have to worry about. In fact, this might be the only place Maddie could be hidden in Chicago where we won't stand out." I have no idea what she's talking about, and from the way everyone else just blinks at her, they don't, either. She throws up her hands. "It's a *school*. The people around Maddie are students. It's exactly where we're supposed to be. Perfect camouflage."

Relief washes over me, and, with it, exhaustion. Between not getting a lot of sleep the night before and finally having a real meal, I am having trouble staying awake.

I pull out my sleeping bag, set it up a little bit away from where the others are still talking, and get in. I'm glad they are happy, but I can't stop worrying. Rosie's right: it's a school. It almost all seems too — easy. I don't like the fact that we don't have a plan.

Maybe that's why, despite how tired I am, I toss and turn. In my dreams I hear the phone ringing in my parents' house. It echoes through the empty rooms, hopelessly, until the echo becomes Troy's voice saying, *The smell, the noise.* "What?" I ask him, but he just looks disappointed at me. And then all I see is his one eye peering at me, and I'm convinced someone is watching me. I try to run but I don't know which way to go, and I can't find my compass, and I open my mouth to scream but there's a hand over it and a voice says, "Stop fighting and be quiet."

Only it's not a dream. Someone really whispers that in my ear. Someone has their hand over my mouth.

Someone crouching right next to me.

My eyes fly open and in the semidarkness the first thing I see is the silver star winking on the sleeve of an Alliance uniform.

Chapter 12

The second thing I see is Helen's face.

She whispers, "If you value your friends' lives, you'll come with me quietly. Do you understand?"

I nod.

She pulls me up by the wrist, not roughly, and leads me from the car wash into the cool night air. There's a tarp on the ground and a pack suspended from an old drainpipe.

"Sit," she says.

"You're camping out here?" I ask.

She puts her finger to her lips. "We have to be quiet. I don't want to wake the others." She follows my eyes and realizes I'm staring not at her but at the Alliance uniform.

She thumbs the collar. "Don't look at me like that. This is yours."

"I told you, we stole it."

"I know. I believe you now. I'm just wearing it for warmth."

It's freezing out in the open. "What are you doing here?" I ask her in a whisper. "Where's Troy? What do you mean about waking the others?"

"He went on alone," she says, with a finality that makes me think I shouldn't ask any more questions. "I decided to follow you. I woke you up first because you seem the most . . . reasonable. Your other leader, the dark-haired angry girl —"

"Rosie?" I manage to say through chattering teeth.

"Yes. I didn't think she'd listen. But you will. And then the others will listen to you."

I'm too cold to be flattered.

She tosses me a hat and some gloves. "Here, put these on."

I pull the hat low over my ears and tuck my hands under my arms. Helen sits down next to me and draws her legs up, wrapping her arms around them. As she shifts I see a flash of yellow at her neck. Like a scarf.

"That was you!" I exclaim. "In the Settlement Lands, you're the one who threw that smoke bomb."

"I thought you could use some help."

"Why did you decide to be our ally?"

She holds up a hand. "I'm not your ally. I didn't follow you because I wanted to help. I followed you to head you off if you tried to turn us in. I couldn't risk you figuring out where we came from and reporting us, or you turning out to be scouts."

That word again. "What's a scout?" I ask.

Her head goes up and down. "Yeah. That's one of the things you're going to need to know about."

"Know about for what?"

"To get your friend away from Phoenix." She stares out at the night. "The plan you have, to go up there, look around, blend in? That's not going to work."

"Wait, you were listening to us?" I ask, and she nods, but I don't have time to focus on that now. "Why isn't it going to work?" I ask instead.

She bites the inside of her cheek, like she's trying to figure out how best to put something. "The way Phoenix is organized, everyone watches everyone else all the time. They'll say 'watches out for' but it's really much more evil. If a cadet — that's what the students are called — sees something out of the ordinary, he or she is supposed to blow the whistle on it. Even if it's a friend. And I'm not talking meteorically; I mean for real."

"Metaphorically," I suggest.

A muscle in her jaw tightens. "Whatever. What I mean is, it's a real whistle that brings real guards. The cadets are told it's a game, to help others be better Phoenix citizens, by helping them remember to follow the rules. The more people you can blow the whistle on, the more points you get. Points lead to privileges and promotion."

"But it's not a game," I say.

"No," Helen agrees, shaking her head. "And part of the way it works is that everyone is supposed to know everybody else. There's no way for you to blend in, especially not all of you. One, maybe two of you could pretend to be new students or transfers, but not all six, not all at once. And since you'd be likely to be challenged, you'd need to know all the Recitations."

I move to sit on my hands for extra warmth. "What are those?"

"The Phoenix motto, the creed, the founding principles. 'Submission is strength.' 'Belonging is beautiful.' 'The group is good.' That kind of thing." She shudders, but not, I think, from the cold.

"If students are called 'cadets,' what are scouts?"

"Scouts are the more advanced cadets, the ones who show the most enthusiasm. Inside Phoenix, they watch out for anyone who might make trouble. And outside, if a cadet doesn't perform properly on a mission or leaves without permission, scouts are sent to bring them back. They're spies." She says the word like it leaves a bad taste on her tongue, and it reminds me of what happened in the Settlement Lands earlier.

"That's why that kid, Bailey, said it that way," I say as much to myself as to her.

"Yeah. No one likes scouts except scouts." She's staring into the night, like part of her is somewhere else. "They'll try to trick you into trusting them, too, like by not wearing their badges, or trick you into doing something wrong just so they can take you in."

"Why would anyone want to be a scout?"

"If you believe in Phoenix, then being a scout is an honor. It means you belong somewhere; you have a place and a purpose. You probably can't understand that but for some of us, that's — It can be appealing."

"I understand the appeal of knowing where you stand," I say.

She looks at me like she doubts it but goes on. "Troy and I thought you and your friends were scouts to start with."

"What changed your mind?"

She looks at me squarely. "Phoenix Center is a place for bad kids. Really bad kids. No offense, but you and your friends aren't tough enough or ruthless enough. You're not Phoenix material."

I can't imagine Maddie with kids like that.

"And there is just something about the way you all are together. You don't wait for each other to mess up. You're — nice." She picks up a stick and draws lines in the dirt next to her foot. "I don't know about this girl you're trying to rescue —"

"She's like us. She's not a bad kid, either."

"Then you better get her out fast. Because it just gets worse the longer you are there."

"She was classified as AL-five. Do you know what that means?"

Helen pauses in her drawing. "Are you sure about your friend? That she's just a good, normal kid?"

"Yes, why?"

"'AL' means Asset Level — how important you are to Phoenix. Which means to the Alliance. Everyone starts at level one or two, depending on what kind of useful abilities you have. As you progress through the Phoenix classes, you move up levels. But I've never known anyone above a level four. Level five is like —" She fans her hand in the air at some mythical height of achievement. "Your friend must have some special skills. It also means they'll be watching her extra closely."

I ransack my brain to think of anything that would set Maddie apart like that. She was okay at putting up a tent, but that doesn't seem like such a big deal. Or maybe Alonso was right. Maybe it has something to do with Maddie's dad.

I say, "The other thing on her record was that she's being moved somewhere called Bright Spa tomorrow. Would it be easier for us to get her from there?"

Before I'm done saying the words, the color has drained from Helen's face. "I had a friend who was moved to Bright Spa. They said it was for medical tests. She didn't come back."

Well, that takes care of that.

"Troy said the only way out of Phoenix is through the chute," I say, pressing on.

"That was the only way we could think of. But you won't be able to do that again. I'm sure they've closed it up. And frankly," she says, still fiddling with her stick, "getting out will be the easy part."

"What do you mean?" I ask. I have the feeling she's avoiding my eyes.

"You'll be spotted as fakes at some point, and once you are, there will be a general scramble with everyone trying to catch you. Phoenix is built on maintaining order. The one thing it isn't designed to deal with is full-scale chaos. You shouldn't have trouble getting away in the middle of it."

I feel myself brightening. "That's good news. So if getting out is the easy part, what's the hard part?"

"Getting in." She continues sketching with her stick. "And I'm afraid I can't help you with that."

I feel completely chilled, but I don't know if it's from the cold or her words. "What *can* you help with?"

"I can tell you what you'll need to know if you get inside, and to keep from getting spotted right away. But there's a lot to learn. It will take two or three days."

I look at the sky. I don't see a hint of dawn yet but it can't be that far away. "We probably have about five hours."

"Then we'd better get started," she says, and stands.

"Why are you helping us?" I ask as we circle around to the front of the car wash.

"Because no one should have to stay at the Phoenix Center," she says, and I think she means it. But I also don't think it's the whole answer.

•   •   •

I decide to wake the others by gently shaking them rather than shining flashlights in their faces and yelling, "On your feet!" which is Helen's suggestion.

"Do what you want, but you're the one with the schedule to keep," she says, slouching against the wall.

I start with Rosie, because I suspect she'll be the most, well, volatile.

"You have got to be kidding," she says, instantly alert. "We can't trust a word she says. That girl is a thief and a sneak."

"Which is why she can help us," I reason. "She's been inside."

Rosie glares in Helen's direction. "She's setting us up."

"Maybe. But since this is our only shot at getting Maddie, we might as well listen to her. Besides, Helen is the one who saved us in the Settlement Lands," I add. "She threw the smoke bomb."

Rosie's eyes haven't moved. "Sure, according to her."

It's clear Rosie isn't happy, but she goes along with it. Louisa is easier — hearing Helen has information that might help us find Maddie is enough to convince her. And with the two of them on board, the boys all agree.

Helen makes us line up and stand at Phoenix attention, which means feet together, hands at your sides, shoulders back, eyes at a sixty-degree angle downward.

"That way you see everything from your peripheral vision but don't make eye contact. As much as possible, avoid looking people in the eye," she explains.

The next four hours are exhausting. First Helen tells us an overwhelming number of facts about Phoenix. She says:

"There are two sets of morning classes but your best bet will be to arrive before the first bell. Whatever you do, do not get caught in the halls between classes. All superiors are addressed as 'sir' whether male or female. Touching the outer corner of your eye with your finger can be friendly and mean 'I'm looking out for you,' or threatening and mean 'I'm watching you.' Got that?"

We have no choice but to nod. We have no choice but to get it.

Next Helen observes the way we stand. She yells at us to stand up straighter, raise or lower our chins, stop fidgeting, take our hands out of our pockets, keep our shoulders even.

"I think this is all made up and she's just playing with us," Rosie says out of the corner of her mouth.

"What is that, Cadet Marquez?" Helen demands, getting in Rosie's face.

Marquez is the fake name that Rosie's chosen for herself for our Phoenix mission. All cadets have to spray their names on the backs of their jackets using stencils when they first get to Phoenix. We don't have any paint or stencils, so we're going to be hand-lettering names on our jackets, using black ink, in what will hopefully look the same as the stencils. But we decided not to use our real names. Instead, we'll use the name of a close relative, which should be easy for us to remember. Marquez is Rosie's aunt's last name.

Helen goes on to explain other things, like: never walk around in groups of more than two; don't trust anyone; don't smile.

"Older cadets are allowed to stop you at any moment and demand an answer to any question, including where any other cadet is," she says. "You are supposed to learn to observe others. They say it makes you a good citizen but really you are always watching to report on their behavior. You'll be called in and asked what you saw someone do. The more detailed a report you can give, the happier they are. So you get really good at spying on your neighbors. Or making stuff up."

She paces in front of us. "Everyone will be watching you. Everyone will be hoping you slip up. No one is on your side. Salute!"

We salute.

"You need to be faster and sharper. And those two," she says, pointing at Alonso and Drew. "They can't go. Anyone who is injured is locked in the infirmary ward because injury weakens the team. 'Don't be the weak link' is one of the Recitations."

"We'll stay here with one of the phones," Drew says.

"And maybe Helen will stay with you. To help out if we have any questions." Rosie says. The gleam in her eye is a challenge.

"You still think I'm trying to betray you," Helen

states. "You think if I went with you, I'd blow the whistle and turn you in."

"The thought crossed my mind," Rosie says.

Helen nods with real appreciation. "You're good. If anyone gets in your face, show them that attitude. I may have been wrong about you; you may have what it takes to make it at Phoenix."

Rosie says, "I'll take that as a compliment."

"Yeah. But it doesn't matter; no way I'm going anywhere near there."

Finally Helen makes us practice the Recitations so many times my tongue is tired. "I may never speak again," I say, and I try not to be disheartened by the sort of laughter that comes out of Rosie and Louisa.

We decide that we will divide up into two teams: Drew, Alonso, and Helen at the car wash with one phone; Louisa, Ryan, Rosie, and I at the library with the other. While those of us who will be going to Phoenix hand-letter our jackets with "our" names, we also hash out a plan for getting in.

Rosie isn't sure she likes what we come up with until Helen announces, "That plan stinks."

Rosie nods. "It's a go."

Dawn is breaking, which means if we want to get to Phoenix before morning classes, it's time for us to leave. I'm exhausted but I also feel jangly. It's like a group of mice is inside me, playing the kind of jazz Mr. Peña likes to listen to when he's cooking.

If this works, I realize, I could go home tonight.

I'm thinking about that, biting my nails and gazing out at the changing blue sky of the chilly morning, when I feel a tap on my shoulder. I turn and find Alonso standing there. His big brown eyes have smudges beneath them from lack of sleep.

He pushes the hair on his forehead to one side. "You said we could finish that conversation we were having yesterday."

"What conversation?" I ask, and I don't mean to play dumb because I really don't remember. Then I do remember and I find that suddenly the prospect of walking right into the den of the enemy is appealing by comparison. In fact, I wish I were there right now.

"About me liking someone," he says, completely ignoring the look of panic on my face. "You were right. I do."

"That's none of my business."

"Here," he says, thrusting a folded-up piece of paper into my hand.

"What is it?"

"It's for luck. Don't look at it until you're on the bus." He turns and walks away, hands in his pockets, shoulders kind of slouched, and I can't help it. I think he looks adorable.

I stash the paper he gave me into my pocket and go back to biting my fingernails until Rosie, Louisa, and Ryan join me. We wave to Helen, Drew, and Alonso, who are huddled together over their phone, as if waiting to hear from us already. Then the four of us hike over to the bus stop, keeping our sweatshirts pulled far over our wrists to hide our missing ID bracelets.

The bus driver doesn't seem to think there's anything wrong with four kids boarding first thing in the morning. Louisa's bus pass beeps once for each of us, we sit down, and the bus rumbles down the street.

We're on our way.

I pull the piece of paper Alonso gave me out of my pocket and unfold it. Inside is one of those chalky hearts from the party store. The side facing me is blank but I turn it over. When I read the note, my chest gets tight.

You were right. I do have a crush on someone.

The heart says, IT'S U.

The bus must be extra bumpy because my stomach is acting funny and my skin is weird and prickly all over. I feel alternately hot and cold and like I want to laugh and like there are tears in my eyes, especially when I remember the day before when I told him I knew he liked someone but she didn't like him and —

I drop my head into my hands. I am such a moron.

"Are you okay?" Rosie asks me. I rewrap the heart and shove it quickly back into my pocket.

"Yeah, I'm just nervous."

"Don't be the weak link," she quotes from the Phoenix Recitations.

"I must follow to lead," I answer her. I feel like we should give some kind of secret handshake.

"I'm nervous, too," she says. "I can't wait until this is over."

We're silent for the rest of the ride and I find myself touching my pocket periodically to make sure the paper is still there.

Rosie, Louisa, and Ryan are all clearly on edge when the bus lets us off. We're still a block from the Harold Washington Library aka Phoenix Center but we can see it, its massive brick structure looming in front of us.

Get in. Get Maddie. Get out. That's all we have to do. Simple.

I'm just thinking the building looks impossibly large when Rosie clamps down on my right arm, Louisa clamps down on my left one, and they drag me up the stairs toward the front door.

"Wait!" I yell, putting a dose of outrage into it. "What are you doing? Let me go! What —"

"Out of our way," Louisa barks at the cadets standing on the stairs, staring. I turn to glance at her and the scowl she's wearing makes her nearly unrecognizable. "We've got a flier! Let us through."

Chapter 13

The cadets step aside, gazing jealously at Rosie, Louisa, and Ryan. Bringing in a flier will earn them five points each and be written into their record. Helen told us all about it.

"Where are your scout badges?" demands a girl with milky-white skin and straight hair the color of corn. She has big blue eyes but they look hard and mean. I see that her nails have chipped black polish on them as she raises her fingers to fiddle with her whistle.

"Where they won't tip the flier off," Louisa says with a curl of her lip that's scary. She's kind of good at this.

The girl's fingers leave the whistle but she doesn't move.

Rosie gives her a fierce stare. "Is your name Mat?"

The girl's eyes narrow. "No."

"Then get out of my way before I walk over you," Rosie says, and muscles us past her. The double doors marked READMISSION slide open with a pneumatic *whoosh* for us to go through.

The secretary on the other side is totally uninterested in us. "Take the flier to reconditioning room one," she says, without looking up from her computer. There are three sets of doors in this room, all solid wood. The secretary pushes a button beneath her desk and the door marked MAIN CAMPUS clicks open.

We're in.

Now we just need to avoid attracting attention. Rosie and Louisa let go of my arms and we all assume the eyes-forward, shoulders-straight posture Helen drilled into us. I can't see a clock so I don't know how long we have until the first bell rings, but the halls are full of kids. They are like the kids at CMS except everyone seems more serious and guarded. No one makes eye contact, but they all watch one another out of the corners of their eyes. When they pass they'll nod or give a low wave but nothing more.

There are no groups of kids joking or hanging out together. I hear Helen's voice. *The more people you trust, the more people can betray you. Cadets usually travel alone or in pairs.*

A boy and a girl are talking to each other, leaning against the wall, but they're not looking at each other. Instead they're watching everyone else as they pass and not, like in normal school, to see what they're wearing or whom they're talking to. More to see if they're engaging in Reportable Behavior.

Rosie blends in pretty well. But even though she's trying to look mean, Louisa's excitement about being this close to finding Maddie seems to be coming off of her in waves. I'm terrified someone will notice.

Don't do anything at first, Helen said. *Be sure no one is paying unusual attention to you before trying to find your friend. And don't trust anyone.*

A guy with skin a little lighter than mine and a crew cut falls into step next to Louisa. "Are you new, Cadet March? I don't remember seeing you before."

Louisa frowns like she's wondering whom he is

talking to. Apparently she's forgotten that her grand-mother's last name was March.

"Transferred in from upstate a few days ago," Rosie answers for her. "Right, Cadet *March*?"

Louisa remembers her fake name. "Oh yeah. Right."

"Ah, that explains the looking around like you've never seen the place before," he says, eyes still on Louisa. He's got the confidence of someone who thinks he's handsome. And maybe he could be under other circum-stances. "Can I help you find anything?"

Louisa blurts, "Do you know where Madeleine Frye is? Um, Cadet Frye?"

There's a flash of surprise in the guy's eyes, and then a calculating expression. "I don't. Who's that?"

"A friend from up north," Rosie rushes to say. "We transferred together."

The guy's eyes move beyond Rosie to me, and then to Ryan behind us. He rubs a hand over his crew cut. I sense him making a note of how many of us there are, and I fall back slightly so it might not look like I'm with them.

"Sorry I can't help," he says. "I'll stay alert." He taps his eye.

Rosie taps her eye back. "Thanks."

He turns and disappears into the crowd behind us. Louisa whispers, "I'm sorry. I wasn't thinking."

"You have to be more careful," Rosie hisses back.

Louisa's shoulders sag slightly. At least now she is looking appropriately miserable.

"I know. Do you think he believed it?" she whispers.

As though answering her question, a whistle shrills behind us. Everyone stops and turns toward it.

My heart is pounding so loud I'm afraid everyone can hear it. Ryan and I are standing next to each other with Rosie and Louisa behind us now. I sense more than see Ryan plant his feet with purpose as though to say anyone who wants to mess with Louisa will have to go through him.

Around us the air simmers with excitement.

Rubber soles squelch up the corridor as a tall, sallow guy with dark hair and dark eyes comes toward us, spinning the whistle around his finger. He's with a shorter but beefier guy with a shaved head and a nose that looks like it has seen some action. Neither of them is the guy with the crew cut who talked to Louisa, but I see him farther down the corridor looking amused.

I hear Helen's voice in my head.

If something happens, if you think they're on to you, take off. Don't give them the opportunity to get close. They're faster than you are and meaner than you are and you won't stand a chance.

The sallow guy and the Nose continue walking toward us, and it feels like they are both staring right through me. I keep my eyes straight ahead but shift my weight onto my heels and get ready to run.

"Cadet Berger, where are your hands?" the sallow one's voice demands.

In my mind I call up the memory of writing the fake names on our hoodies — Rosie is Marquez, Louisa is March, I am Weinberg, and Ryan is —

"In my pockets," a voice croaks in front of me, and I glance down and see a short boy, probably only three feet tall, with curly light brown hair.

179

The sallow guy's expression is mean, but he licks his lips like he's getting ready to enjoy himself.

"And where should they be?"

The little boy answers, "By my sides." It comes out as more of a squeak. He's clearly terrified.

"What is the Phoenix motto?"

"My future. My fate. My hands," the boy recites.

"Your future sure is your hands," the sallow boy says with a low, mean laugh. The Nose snorts and they start off, the sallow one adding as an afterthought, "At ease, Cadet."

Their path takes them past us and the sallow one brushes against Ryan's shoulder. Ryan flinches and the Nose stops in front of him. "What are you looking at, Cadet?"

"Nothing, sir," Ryan replies, gaze down. I see his fists flexing.

Out of the corner of my eye I see a dozen hands move instantly toward their whistles. Calling in the guards on a fight is an easy way to get points.

The Nose keeps staring at Ryan, chest out, like he's daring Ryan to make a move, any move. Ryan's neck and ears are turning red but he stays completely still. I'm not even sure he's breathing. I don't know how he stands it but somehow he does.

Finally the sallow kid says, "Come on, Emile. We've had our fun for the day."

The bully's name is Emile! No wonder he's so mean.

They continue by and the hands drop from the whistles and everyone goes back to what they were doing.

"Well done," I whisper to Ryan. He doesn't say anything; he's still clenching his jaw.

"I want to get out of here," Rosie says, and I've never seen her with the expression she has on her face. A guy our age goes by and she barks at him, "Attention!" He stops and salutes her, and she demands, "Do you know the location of Cadet Frye?"

"No, sir. I regret I do not, sir."

"I do," his friend says. He isn't standing at attention. "I'll tell you for a smile."

"I'll write you up for impudence, Cadet — What's his name?" Rosie demands of the other one, who is still saluting.

"Greene, sir," the saluting one offers, turning on his friend without blinking an eye.

"Cadet Greene, what is the location of Cadet Frye?"

"She is in the boiler. Sir," he says, giving a weak salute.

"I have my eye on you," Rosie tells him, making the tapping gesture again. "At ease."

We'd moved slightly apart, and when Rosie rejoins us, she's shaking. "I feel like I need to wash my mouth out."

I nod. Acting like them, having to think like them, is making me feel creepy, too. "The boiler must be in one of the subbasements," I say. "That's where they always are in old buildings."

"Good. Let's figure out which one and get Maddie out of here now," Louisa says, grimly. "I don't even want to think about what she's going through in here."

"We should split up. We'll find her faster," Rosie says.

"But we only have one phone," Ryan objects.

Then the bell rings for morning classes.

Our eyes meet and I know we're all hearing Helen say, *Whatever you do, don't be caught in the hall between classes. And if you have to be, only in groups of two. That way you can pretend one of you is escorting the other some-where for punishment.*

"We have no choice," Rosie says urgently to Ryan. "You and Louisa go left. Evelyn and I will go right. I'll keep the phone. The next bell rings in forty-five minutes. If we don't meet in the boiler, we make our way to the emergency exit and pull the alarm then, with or without Maddie. Got it?"

I really don't like that last part and I can see by the expression on Louisa's face she doesn't, either. But Rosie is right. We have no choice.

After a moment Ryan nods and Louisa says, "Got it," and they disappear into the crowd filing down the stairs to the left. As they go, I am seized with the awful feeling that this could be the last time I see my friends. Any of my friends.

I touch the pocket of my hoodie and feel Alonso's present there. This isn't the time for What's the Worst that Can Happen? thinking. It's the time for action.

Rosie and I go down a long corridor. As we make our way toward the stairs at the end, I glance at the class-rooms. I remember Helen describing the classes as "cool and not boring like regular school" and I see right away these are nothing like the classrooms at CMS. One of them has a table with what looks like power tools on it. Another one has a car parked in the middle. A third room has a red light above the door next to the words TOXIC MATERIALS LABORATORY: OBSERVE ALL POISON PROTOCOLS WHEN LIT. A fourth has electrical boxes on each desk that remind me of lie detector machines I've seen in old movies.

"Stop gaping," Rosie says to me through clenched teeth. "You're looking too interested."

A quick glance around shows me she's right. A guy with a long braid trailing over his shoulder is watching us, fingers idly toying with his whistle. Two girls with identical pink-and-white-dotted headbands keep glancing in our direction and then turning and whispering to each other.

"I think I know what animals at the zoo must have felt like," I whisper to Rosie.

"At the zoo they didn't hunt the animals," she whispers back.

A girl with a curtain of dark hair falling over her face gives me a shy glance as we walk by. Without thinking I smile at her. She smiles back. I feel a little better. Maybe not everyone here is bad.

We finally reach the stairs and join the stream of people flowing down to the first floor. The stairs dead-end there, and that hallway is quickly emptying as everyone files into their classrooms.

"There's an exit sign ahead." Rosie speaks so low her lips barely move. "There must be more stairs there. We'll make for it and —"

"Halt!" a voice says from behind us. "Cadets, stop where you are."

I look around and realize we're the only ones in the corridor.

"Don't stop," Rosie urges. "Keep going to the —"

"I said, halt!" the voice commands, and it's followed by a strong hand on our shoulders.

We turn slowly and find ourselves face-to-face with a tall, muscular guy with a scar through his eyebrow, a tattoo on his neck, and a Scout Supervisor badge. "What do you think you're doing out of class?" he demands. His eyes are mean and appraising.

I swallow hard. "I'm a flier and she is taking me —" I start to say.

That's when Rosie reaches out and slaps him across the face.

Chapter 14

I'm pretty sure that isn't what Helen meant about showing attitude. Especially when Rosie adds, "You liar! Murderer! Traitor!" and starts hitting him with her fists.

"Whoa, Rosie, calm down," he says. Over her head he looks at me. "Little help here?"

Somewhere between thinking, *What is Rosie doing?* and *You need to stop this!* my brain hears what he said.

"How did you know Rosie's name?" I ask him.

"This is Ivan," Rosie says, socking him hard in the stomach. He staggers backward. "The guy who betrayed my sister to the Alliance and got her killed."

Ah. Well, that explains it.

"I didn't," Ivan the betrayer hisses, grasping his midsection. "It's not what you think."

I look at him, and I'm pretty sure my expression matches Rosie's, which is Steely in the Extreme.

"I'm not Alliance," he says.

Rosie moves toward him and pulls back a fist. "That's weird because you sure look —"

"Wren is alive," he tells Rosie. That stops her like she's been frozen in nitrogen.

"How do you know? Where is she?"

"We can't talk here; it's not safe. Come with me."

Rosie makes a noise that I think is meant to be laughter but sounds like a growl. "So you can turn us in?"

"I swear. I'm here on a mission for the Resistance. Obviously I'm too old to be a student so they had me assigned as a scout supervisor so I could infiltrate."

"Liar. The Resistance has never heard of Ivan Franks," Rosie snarls at him.

"Of course they said that; they're protecting me." His eyes dart behind us, then go back to her. "You don't think they just give out the names of their members, do you? We really need to go somewhere else." He's looking truly nervous now and it dawns on me that there's something strange about what he's saying: it has that weird sound that only one thing has. The truth.

I make a gut decision. "Rosie, I believe him," I say.

An expression of betrayal flashes across Rosie's face, replaced by fury. "How can you —"

"Trust me," I say to her. For some reason I see Alonso's face, saying the same words to me. "Just — trust me."

Rosie looks from me to Ivan and back to me.

"You're sure?" she asks, her hands still clenched into fists.

I nod. "Plus, having him along will make it easier for us to be in the halls."

And then the most amazing thing happens. She says, "Okay."

Just like that. Just because I said it.

Ivan says, "I know a safe place we can talk."

"We don't have time to talk," Rosie says. "We're here to find our friend Maddie and you're going to help us, traitor."

Ivan exhales hard. "I told you —"

"She's in the boiler," I say. "We need to get her out."

Ivan's forehead furrows. "You think you are going to get someone out of here? Not likely. Especially not if she's on boiler duty."

"Yes, we are," Rosie says. "And while we do it, you're going to tell me where Wren is and when you saw her last and how I can find her."

I am not liking Ivan's tone or expression. "What is special about boiler duty?" I ask him.

"It's assigned to the best cadets," he says. "Meaning the most obedient ones. It's an honor. No one on a boiler will want to leave."

"Maddie will," I say.

Ivan shakes his head. "Even if you can convince her, you can't just walk out of here. Phoenix is heavily secured."

"We know that, traitor," Rosie says. I am thinking she might want to stop reminding him of the traitor part. But she's got her Really Angry Face on and is in one of those moods where she looks like she has the power of six women, so I don't want to antagonize her. Now she adds, "We're going to make a ruckus and create chaos. Chaos is what Phoenix isn't built for."

"Sure, yeah." Ivan nods. "And that's why they have full lockdown capability. At the first sign of disruption, the entire facility can be sealed in ninety seconds. One person might get out. Possibly two. But not three, no way."

"What about five?" I say.

"There are more of you?" He peers closely at us as though we might have been hiding people in our clothes. "What, did you bring a band or something?"

"That's on a need-to-know basis," Rosie says. She shifts her Angry Face to me. "Your friend Helen didn't mention we had less than two minutes to get out."

"No." I try to sound light and unconcerned. "Maybe that's what she meant by 'plan to leave fast.'"

Rosie snarls, "Let's call her and ask." She pulls the phone from her pocket.

For such a big guy, it takes almost no time for all the color to drain from Ivan's face. "You can't use that in here," he croaks. "Cadets aren't allowed to have phones, and they'll trace any signal instantly. They could even be tracking it now."

Rosie eyes him speculatively. "So that's the line you're going to use when they find us."

Ivan throws up his hands. "Fine. Don't listen to me." To me he says, "The lockdown procedure is new in the last week. They've been upgrading security for the past month. Something is going on, something big. That's why the Resistance planted me."

I feel better knowing Helen is (probably) not a liar but that doesn't help with our exit strategy.

He goes on. "My mission here is extremely important. I can't do anything that might blow my cover. It's great you want to get your friend Maxie but —"

Rosie reaches up, grabs Ivan by the collar, and pulls his face down so they are standing eye to eye. "Maddie," she pronounces carefully. "Her name is Madeleine Frye. And there is no 'but.' We're going to get her. And you are going to help us."

Either Maddie's name or Rosie's tone has a strange effect on Ivan. Everything about him seems more alert and engaged. "Madeleine Frye is on boiler duty," he says, and it's not clear if it's a question or a statement.

Rosie releases him. "For now. Until she's moved to Bright Spa."

"Do you know Maddie?" I ask, trying to puzzle out the change in him.

"No," Ivan says, and again I think he's telling the truth. So why does he suddenly care?

"What is the meaning of this noise, Supervisor?" A gray-haired woman in a floral dress pokes her head into the hallway from a classroom. She looks like a grandma from an old TV show, small and frail with bright eyes that dart around like a tiny bird. "We are trying to do real work in here."

"I'm sorry, Miss Castle." Ivan speaks deferentially. "I'm taking these two cadets to the boiler."

"Then take them, young man," Miss Castle says with a wave of her hand, and ducks her head back into her classroom.

"What does she teach?" I ask as Ivan walks us to the staircase.

"Hand-to-hand combat. She can kill you with her pinkie."

I look at him to see if he is joking, but he isn't.

"Where is Wren?" Rosie demands as we run down another set of stairs.

"I don't know," Ivan says. "I really don't know."

"Liar."

"It's true, although even if I did, I might not tell you."

"Why?"

"Wren is working for the Resistance. She's doing what she wants. She knew the price of it was that she'd have to cut off contact with her family."

Rosie's jaw tightens. "She didn't know."

"Yes, Rosie. She did."

Rosie's hand starts to make a fist again. "She wouldn't have done that. You're a liar."

"This is a war. Sometimes you have to make hard choices to do what's right."

"I don't need you to tell me about hard choices, traitor," Rosie growls at him.

We have reached Subbasement 2 now and I hear a strange, windy noise.

"What's that?" I ask.

"We're getting close to the boiler," Ivan says. "Two more levels."

At the next set of stairs the sound has changed. It's louder but it sounds more . . . human. And I smell something. Something burning.

"Are they incinerating their garbage?" I ask. That's strictly forbidden by the Environmental Statutes, but it's the kind of dirty thing the Alliance would do.

"They would describe it as garbage, yes. You might have a different opinion," Ivan replies cryptically. We're on Subbasement 3 now, but instead of continuing down he takes us onto a metal catwalk. It rings a vast open space, the size of a sports stadium.

"Oh, man," Rosie breathes.

In rows stretching as far as we can see are round metal tanks, fifty or sixty of them, spewing fire. Next to each of them is a trolley filled with books. As I watch, the cadet below us opens a big, clothbound volume that looks like the old dictionary Alonso found. The cadet rips off the cover. There's a strange noise like the sound of the wind whistling through tall grass as she drops it in the fire. An orange flame leaps up with a *whoosh* when she throws in the pages. She smiles as she watches them burn.

I feel like I'm going to be sick.

"Welcome to the boiler," Ivan says.

Chapter 15

My knuckles on the railing are white from gripping it so hard.

"Books?" Rosie asks. "They're burning books for fuel? They couldn't find anything else?"

Ivan gives a bitter laugh. "These fires don't generate power or even heat for the building. They're burning these books just to destroy them."

My eyes sting and I don't know whether from the smoke or from outrage. "But why? And why is this assigned to top cadets?"

Ivan turns his back on the boiler and faces us. "Because they're the ones heralding in a new world order. Getting rid of the dangerous old ideas. Some of it is just symbolic until they can destroy the digi-files. But many of these are from the rare book collections and haven't been uploaded."

I can't believe I heard him right. "These are — these are things people spent lifetimes learning, going up in smoke. For — nothing. It's barbaric. It's —" I don't even have the words.

"I see her." Rosie leans over the railing. She points far ahead to the left. "Down there. I see Maddie."

My heart leaps. "We've got to get her out of here," I say. "Now."

"This way." Ivan leads us around the edge of the catwalk to a ladder. There must have been some kind of ventilation around the catwalk because even though heat rises, it seems to get hotter as we go down. The sides of the ladder are coated but it's still hot under my touch, and I pull my sleeves up over my hands to keep from getting burned. Breathing the overheated air leaves my nose and throat raw.

When we get to the bottom, Ivan says, "I have to go check on something," and vanishes before Rosie can object.

The heat on the floor makes the air shimmer. Then I see her.

Even with the familiar messy brown ponytail on top of her head and the name FRYE stenciled on her jacket, it takes me a moment to believe that the girl with her back to us is really Maddie. That we really found her.

It's much louder down here so she doesn't hear us rush to her, and Rosie is hugging her before Maddie even knows what's happening. She's so surprised that she narrows her brown eyes and glares at us. But when Rosie lets her go, Maddie doesn't stop glaring.

Then the glare softens to confusion. "What are you doing here?" she asks.

"We came to rescue you," I say.

Rosie reaches for Maddie's arm. "Come on."

"Rescue me?" Maddie looks from one to the other of us. There's something different about her. Like something is missing. "From what?"

"From this place," I say. "From —" I look down and I see that Maddie is holding the leather cover of a book. It was once beautiful, nubby red leather with gold swirls making a border. On the spine I can still read the words *Collected Works of P. Virgilius.* But the pages are gone.

Maddie's eyes follow mine and she tosses the cover into the boiler. Down here, the sound it makes when it burns isn't like whistling; it's higher-pitched. I know now what Troy meant when he said they shriek like you're stealing their souls.

Maddie reaches to take another book from her trolley, and without thinking I go to stand in front of it.

"Please move. I have a task to accomplish," she says.

My brows come together in a frown. "That's what you call this? A task?"

"Making way for the new. We have to return to basics. Start fresh. These books just hold a lot of old ideas that don't work. The same way the phoenix rose from the ashes of its former self, the new world will rise from the ashes of the old."

"That doesn't even make sense," I say. I'm sure she can't really believe what she's saying. "For one thing, the phoenix is a myth, and for another —"

Maddie nods her head like I am making her point for her. "That is all learning is good for: arguing. We don't need arguments and questions. We need consensus and answers. Questions make us weak. Agreement makes us strong."

I feel like my ears are playing tricks on me. I can't really be hearing what I seem to be hearing. "But what about the freedom to think what you want?"

Maddie blinks at me with her strange, dead eyes. "Where has always questioning everything gotten you, Evelyn? Did it make you happy?"

"It helped us find you," I say. I've curled my fingers into fists to keep my hands from shaking. This is impossible. She's been here less than a week. How could they have taken over her mind so completely?

Maddie shrugs. "Maybe you shouldn't have bothered."

Rosie says, "We have to go, Maddie."

Now Maddie shifts her empty gaze to Rosie. "I don't want to go. This is the first place I've really felt like I belong. In here I don't need to lie about who I am or what my name is or who my parents are. They treat me like *I'm* important. Like I, Madeleine Frye, can make a difference. This is where I'm supposed to be."

A tall, very skinny boy materializes through the smoke to stand next to Maddie. He's got unruly longish brown hair and his eyes are only halfway open.

"Cadet Frye, is everything okay?" he asks. He brushes a hair off Maddie's forehead protectively.

Rosie and I both tense.

"Yes." Maddie smiles up at him, but even that seems somehow tepid. "Hi, Jonah, um, Cadet Carson. These are my friends. From that other school."

"The rich kids," Jonah says, nodding. He hooks his thumbs through the belt holes of his pants, which at least is not near his whistle. "Yeah, I heard about your crew. What are you doing here?"

"We, um, came to, um —" I find I'm having trouble forming the words.

"They came to rescue me," Maddie says.

The Jonah guy gives Maddie a half-bemused smile. "You don't need rescuing, do you, Cadet?" he asks.

Maddie slowly shakes her head, kind of like she's mesmerized. "No. I am proud to be a Phoenix cadet," she says in a weird, impersonal voice.

Jonah looks from her to us, and his expression is almost pitying. "That's how it always is with *them*. They think everyone wants what they do."

"We're not the ones who make everyone recite weird mottos," Rosie points out. "We're not the ones doing the brainwashing."

"Brainwashing?" Jonah looks confused.

By the curl in her lip, it's clear that Rosie likes Jonah even less than I do. She turns from him back to Maddie. "I thought friendship was about trust and helping each other out. If this place is so friendly, why is everyone always trying to turn everyone else in?"

In that same weird voice, Maddie says, "We are being trained to spot threats and neutralize them. To serve our country."

"How? By spying on your neighbors?" Rosie challenges.

This is going horribly wrong. "We're not here to make you do anything," I say fast. My lip is quivering and I feel like I might cry. "We — Maddie, you're our friend. We were worried about you."

Maddie makes a big gesture with her arms. "Well, look around. I'm fine. So you don't have to worry."

"But —" I don't know what else to say.

There's a thunderous running and out of nowhere Louisa appears, with Ryan close behind her. Louisa throws her arms around Maddie's neck.

"Maddie oh my god I thought we'd lost you and we almost died and then just now a scout almost caught us and we ran down the first stairs and they led here and thank god, thank god, let's go." She starts pulling her back toward the catwalk.

"This one must be Louisa," Jonah says. And not in a nice way. In a way that kind of makes me want to hit him. He doesn't even glance at Ryan, standing next to her.

I sense Maddie hesitate. She stares at Louisa, and I think we might be getting through to her. But then she says, "Yeah," and pushes Louisa away, toward Ryan. "I was just telling the rest of your friends that I'm not coming with you. This is where I belong. I'm happy here."

Louisa is gaping and her eyes are big blue saucers. "*My* friends? They're your friends, too. You have no idea how hard we all worked to find you."

Maddie's chin goes into the air. "I have new friends now."

Louisa's normally happy face goes slack, and it looks like she is going to sob. Ryan moves toward her but she shakes her head and says, "Maddie — it's . . . me. It's Louisa. You can't be happy here. Everyone is so mean."

"Yeah, not like at CMS, where even you were mean to me."

Louisa takes an unsteady step backward and cups her hand around the place where her locket had been. Maddie's expression wavers and for a split second I see the girl I remember. I decide to take advantage of it.

I say, "Maddie, these people aren't your friends and this isn't your home. It's run by the Alliance."

She shifts her eyes to me and there's a small, sarcastic smile on her lips. "Coming from you, Evelyn, that's not exactly a fact. I think I would know."

I feel like I've been slapped. Maddie was one of the only people who listened to me before. She was my favorite thing about CMS. And now the way she's looking at me is like . . . we're enemies.

Louisa is standing to one side, lost in her own world, and I'm having trouble speaking. So it's up to Rosie to say, "We met a brother and sister named Helen and Troy who escaped from here, and they told us all about it. About it being an Alliance place and the motto and the Recitations. 'Submission is strength.' 'I must follow to lead.' That's not you, Maddie."

Maddie's eyes flicker from Rosie to Jonah.

"I heard about a brother and sister like that," Jonah says with a shrug. "But they were bad cadets and got expelled."

"That's not true," I tell them. "They both worked a boiler."

"Anyone can *say* that," Maddie points out.

"They didn't say it. I saw it: The front of their hair was ragged and short. Because it got singed by the fire."

Maddie reaches up unconsciously and runs her finger over her hairline, where a few shorter pieces are already poking up. I can tell she's starting to at least hear what I'm saying, but she still looks cold. Shuttered. I glance at Louisa to see if she can help but she's staring at the ground. Ryan is next to her, leaning close like he's trying to comfort her.

"I can't take this," I hear Rosie say, and when I turn toward her I see she's covering her face with her hands. She takes a long, ragged breath.

"What's wrong with her?" Maddie asks. Her tone is abrupt but her eyes look concerned.

Rosie lowers her hands and there are tears streaking her face. I'm shocked. Her expression holds such genuine misery that my heart hurts.

"We've done nothing but look for you, and then when we find you — you — you hate us. It's like my sister, Wren. She chose not to see us anymore. She *chose* that. She left me. I can't face losing anyone else." Now Rosie starts to cry for real and I move to hug her.

But Maddie is there first.

She puts her arms around Rosie, and in that moment she looks like our Maddie again. "I'm sorry about your sister," Maddie says. "I'm sure she had a good reason."

"For the War. To fight," Rosie says into Maddie's shoulder. "And I understand but it's just, I miss her. I miss her so much. You know what it's like. You're the only one who understands that."

Maddie stiffens and starts to pull away and I see the curtain start to fall back into place.

Rosie must sense it, too, because she grabs Maddie by the shoulders and pleads. "Please come with us. Everything Evelyn has said is true. This is an evil place. Do you really want to work for the Alliance? Work against your parents?"

Maddie pulls all the way back but Rosie seems to have struck a chord. Whatever was masking Maddie's emotions is gone, but it's been replaced by confusion so intense it looks like fear.

"Don't say that!" Maddie cries, shaking her head. Her tone is different, more like the old Maddie and I see

Louisa look up as Maddie goes on. "It's a lie. This isn't an Alliance school. I'm not working against my parents. My parents *want* me here. The headmistress told me when I arrived. If I pass cadet training at the top of my class, I'll get to see them."

That's why she was so eager to believe, I realize. That's why she went along with everything.

Ivan steps out from between two of the boilers. "They may have said that but it's not true." I wonder how long he's been lurking there and what he had to "check."

Maddie's hand flies to her whistle and she takes a step backward. "Who's this?"

"Who's that?" Louisa asks as she and Ryan move closer to us.

"He's with us," I tell her.

"But how —" Ryan begins.

Ivan interrupts him. "We have to go."

Maddie is gripping her whistle. "Is this a test? Are you — Is this a trap?" She has it halfway to her lips.

"No." I try hard to hold her eyes. "He's helping us."

"He's a scout supervisor. He trains scouts." Maddie's

voice rises with panic. "If this is an Alliance school, why are you working with one of the teachers?"

"He's not a teacher; he's —"

Ivan steps in front of Maddie. "I know your parents. I know one of them very well. They talk about you all the time. I know they call you 'Sparrow.' And I know they would not want you here."

The numbness completely drops from Maddie's face and is replaced with a combination of shock and hope and disbelief. "Where did you see them?" she asks.

"That doesn't matter. We have to go."

"Who are you?"

"Later," Ivan says. "Something is happening. We have to —"

"I don't think so," a high, girlish voice says.

The shy-looking girl with the dark hair that I smiled at in the hallway appears from between two boilers.

"I've been following you all morning," she says in a soft voice. Her eyes are dancing merrily and you can tell she is really enjoying herself. "I've heard *everything*. And now, for capturing four fliers and one Resistance double agent, I am going to be the most famous cadet in Phoenix history." She gives me that same shy smile again and puts the whistle to her lips.

Rosie leaps at her a fraction of a second too late. The whistle shrills and three Phoenix security guards close in on us.

Chapter 16

Rosie marches up to one of the security men and punches him in the stomach.

He doesn't even flinch.

She looks at him, like this doesn't make any sense, and tries it again.

This time he bends down to grab her, and while he's like that, I take the largest book from Maddie's trolley and bring it down on his head.

He staggers forward and falls on his face.

"Reading is hard," Rosie says.

"Knowledge is power," I answer.

These are *not* approved Phoenix Recitations.

The girl with the dark hair is blowing her whistle even louder.

"Someone needs to take that thing away from her," Rosie comments. But before any of us can get to her, Jonah's lifted her up, turned her upside down, and shaken her until the whistle slips from around her neck into the unlit furnace.

"I might have to change my opinion of that guy," Rosie says.

We turn in time to see Ryan run full speed at a second guard, head-butting him. The guard takes a step backward — tripping right over Louisa's waiting leg. The third guard has got one meaty hand clamped on Maddie's shoulder, but as he turns to look at his colleague floundering on the ground, his grip loosens for a split second. Maddie scrambles away and when he lunges to recapture her, Ivan drives the book trolley into his stomach, stopping him cold.

"Move, now," Ivan shouts and takes off in the direction opposite the one through which we entered, with Maddie, Rosie, Louisa, Ryan, Jonah, and me on his heels.

He swerves to activate a fire alarm, then continues on. Sprinklers start dumping water over the boilers and lights begin to flash. A loudspeaker bleats "Fire containment system activated. Proceed to nearest exit."

"Now we only have ninety seconds to get away," I yell over the noise. "I thought you said chaos wouldn't work."

"It won't," Ivan yells back. "But chaos plus the Resistance's secret tunnel might."

Our feet slosh through puddles. "You didn't tell us you had a secret tunnel."

"You didn't tell me who your friend really was." Ivan's eyes are moving over the wall alongside us as we run. Finally he smiles like he's found what he was looking for. All I see is a solid wall with a fire alarm on it.

"What are we —"

Ivan pulls the fire alarm but this time no alarm goes off. Instead the wall shifts soundlessly to create a narrow doorway.

He shepherds all of us through and flips a switch. A line of flickering bulbs mounted in the ceiling quiver to life. We're standing in a square room, with five hallways leading off of it. They have all been painted an unfortunate shade of green but the paint is peeling in spots.

214

"The Resistance built this?" I ask a little nervously. I'm not sure this speaks well of their engineering prowess or decorative schemes.

"Nope, it's part of the original building. I found it when I was studying the old blueprints looking for ways to sneak in," Ivan explains. "I don't think the Alliance knows it's here."

"You don't *think*?" Ryan asks nervously.

"I'm pretty sure. Unfortunately, it's not hard to find and there's no lock. But that one there" — Ivan points to the second tunnel on the right — "is a direct shot to the street. Go straight down to the end of the corridor. The door there leads —"

Rosie holds up her palm. "We're not going without you."

Ivan puts a hand on her shoulder, like a big brother just having a chat with his kid sister. "It's only a matter of time before the guards get through. I'll stay here and make them chase me down the wrong hallway."

"Not a chance." Rosie shakes the hand off. "Your cover is blown and you're the only link I have to my sister."

Ivan looks at me. "This is more important than you realize. You have to get Madeleine Frye out of here."

"I'll stay and stand guard," Jonah volunteers.

Maddie looks stricken. "But if this is an Alliance place, you can't stay, either. You have to come with us." She turns to us, desperate. "He has to come. Jonah saved my life when I first got here."

"Cadet Frye, I order you to go," Jonah tells her. "Just watch. I bet you anything I'll make it."

"You better," Maddie says. She touches the corner of her eye and Jonah does the same.

We hear the distinct sound of footsteps on the other side of the thick wall and someone saying, "I could have sworn it was right here."

"Time to move," Ivan says.

We do. Ivan leads the way, and we follow. The hallway we run down ends in a door with a small painted-over window above it. Ivan uses a key on his belt to unlock the door. He pushes on it; it doesn't budge. There's something blocking it from opening on the other side.

We're trapped.

Behind us the sound of footsteps echoes eerily off the hallway. It's impossible to know if they are close or far away.

"Lift me up," Maddie orders, eyeing the window. "If I can get out, I can clear away whatever's on the other side of the door."

The mere thought of her going through the window makes my palms clammy and ties my stomach in a knot, but I don't say anything.

Ryan and Ivan each take a foot and together they get Maddie to the level of the window clasp. She fiddles with it and finally gets it to turn, but the paint on the window has created a strong seal.

The footsteps are definitely getting closer.

"Loop your whistle over the clasp," Louisa suggests. Without missing a beat, Maddie does it. Louisa leaps up like an ace athlete, grabs the whistle, and dangles from it. The window makes a sound like a sigh, and creaks open.

Maddie smiles down at her. "Nice work, sis."

Louisa shrugs. "We're a good team."

"Yeah," Maddie agrees. She hesitates. "I'm sorry about before. Everything I said. I just — I was —"

Louisa touches the corner of her eye. "No problem."

Rosie gives Maddie a knowing look. "Oh, don't worry; we are so making you pay for how you acted later."

"I figured," Maddie says. "I mean, that's what friends are for, right?" She smiles, waves, and, as though it's no big deal, drops through the window.

Nothing happens.

Behind us I hear the sound of footsteps running.

"Maddie?" Louisa calls, leaning her ear next to the door. "Rosie was just kidding about making you pay."

Nothing.

I swear I can hear the clicking of the handcuffs on the guards' belts now as they rush toward us.

Then the door swings open from outside.

"Come on!" Maddie says.

We are in some kind of walled-in yard filled with the office furniture they'd pulled out of the library. Maddie is scaling a mound of desks and chairs, with Louisa and Ryan after her and me and Rosie after them. I assume Ivan is right behind me but as I get to the top and look back, I see the guards burst through the door and get him by the neck of his jacket.

He wriggles out of it, evading their grasp. Then he turns and hits them with these insane karate-type moves, knocking them both out. The Resistance must have a very good gym because he leaps like a panther onto the pile of furniture and clambers up it.

He, Rosie, and I all drop from the wall at the same time.

We land in an alley behind the library. There are Dumpsters and two delivery vans, one of them with the window rolled down. Ryan reaches in and unlocks the door and opens it.

"We don't have time for —" Rosie is just starting to say as the engine roars to life.

"Hop in," Ryan says.

I can't believe it. "Nice job!"

Ryan turns a little red and whispers, "Don't tell Rosie but the keys were in it."

Louisa goes around to the passenger side and Ivan is in the back wrenching the door open. Maddie and Rosie climb in and I'm about to when Maddie pokes her head back out.

"Where's Jonah? I don't want to go without him."

"Get in," Ivan orders.

"But —"

At that moment Jonah vaults over the wall, with the two guards Ivan had put out of business right on his tail. One of the guards points at Ivan, yells, "That one! Get him!" and they swerve away from Jonah and toward Ivan.

Jonah jumps into the van. Ivan is one second behind him.

Rosie reaches out her hand for him. "Hurry! Get in."

One of the guards lunges for Ivan's leg.

"*Come on!*" Rosie urges.

Ivan leaps and flies through the air, fingers scrambling to grasp the edge of the van. Rosie and I each grab one of his wrists to try to haul him in. Behind him, the two guards latch on to his legs.

"Go!" I scream at Ryan.

"You have to get this to the Hornet," Ivan pants.

"Hold on," Rosie says. "You're coming with us."

"The Hornet," Ivan repeats. His face is bathed in sweat. "The Hornet is Madeleine Frye's mother. Make sure she gets —"

Ryan hits the gas and Ivan lets go. A tiny, light-colored object bounces into the back of the van.

As Rosie and I claw to close the flapping rear doors, we get a last glimpse of Ivan, a guard on each side of him, being dragged backward down the alley. He sees us, too, and yells, "Wren is with her. Find Madeleine's mother and you'll find Wren."

Then the tires squeal and Ryan spins around a corner and the doors of the van slam closed.

"Wren is with the Hornet," Rosie repeats in a daze.

"The Hornet is a woman," I say. "She's . . . she's Maddie's mother."

Maddie looks the most surprised of all. "What does that mean? That my mother is a hornet?"

In the front seat Louisa turns around. Rosie and I both stare at Maddie and I realize she really doesn't know.

"*The* Hornet," I say. "It means that your mother is the leader of the Resistance."

Jonah's mouth falls open.

For a moment I can't tell if Maddie is going to laugh or cry, and I'm not sure Maddie can tell, either.

"My *mom*?" she repeats. "*My* mom?" She stares into space. I'm starting to wonder if any of us knows our parents as well as we think we do.

"Maddie?" Louisa touches her best friend's shoulder. "Maddie, are you okay?"

Now Maddie covers her face with her hands, and lets out a stream of words. "All the times I yelled at her because I felt like she wasn't paying enough attention to me. Because she worked even when she was home on leave. All the times I asked why someone else's parents couldn't go instead of her. Why she couldn't stay with me." Maddie looks up at Louisa, who is draped over the back of the seat. "I didn't tell you this but right before she left the last time she and I had this big fight. I yelled at her and asked why she and my dad couldn't be more like your parents. She said one day I would understand and I told her I did; I understood she didn't love me. Instead of getting mad she just begged me to be patient, but when she left —"

Maddie is crying too hard to keep talking. Louisa climbs over the seat and sits next to her, stretching the sleeve of her sweatshirt over her hand and using it to wipe the tears from Maddie's cheeks.

"Shhh, it's okay," Louisa says.

Maddie, eyes down, shakes her head. "When my mom left, she went to kiss me on the forehead and I pulled away. How could I do that? She is out there trying to save us and I was so selfish I pulled away."

Rosie and I move closer to Maddie and Louisa puts her arms around her. "You didn't know," Louisa says. "You couldn't."

Maddie shudders and wipes her face on her sleeve. "I guess. But I should have." She frowns at Louisa. "I should have known something was going on. I mean, you've

223

eaten my mother's cooking. How could I ever have believed she was an army mess cook?"

Louisa nods solemnly. "That's true. Your mom is the worst cook *ever*. She can't even make a protein shake."

And without warning, Maddie starts to laugh. And then we're all laughing. Laughing the way you can only with your best friends. Laughing because no matter what happens, we're together.

"Stop it," Rosie wails. "I have a stomach cramp."

By the time the laughing has calmed down to random giggles, we all do.

"Okay seriously," Maddie says, trying to make a stern face. "I can't believe it. I just . . . My mom. My mom is —"

"— probably the most important person in the country," I finish for her.

She lets out a long breath. As that sinks in, something changes in Maddie. I don't know if she actually sits up straighter, but she seems to. She nods to herself and says, "Right. Leader of the Resistance. Most important person in the country. Okay." Her head goes from side to side. "Where is that little box the scout supervisor who isn't a scout supervisor threw into the van? The one he said I have to give to my mom?"

Rosie, Louisa, and I feel around beneath us. There's a coil of rope but otherwise it's empty and there's no sign of —

Jonah's been so quiet I'd almost forgotten he was there until he pipes up, "Got it!" He pulls a small, yellowish-white thing from beneath his leg.

Maddie takes it and holds it between two fingers, examining it from all sides. It's a small rectangle of what looks like alabaster, intricately worked in an elaborate pattern of hexagons.

There's something familiar about it. "It's a honeycomb," I say. "But it looks man-made, not like something real bees would make."

"Or hornets," Rosie supplies.

I feel a chill of excitement. "Maybe this is how the Resistance communicates. Maybe it's a message, like a code."

Maddie shakes it near her ear. "It sounds like there's something inside. It could be a box. But I don't see any way to open it." She puts it on the palm of her hand and raises it to the level of her eyes. "What are you?" she asks. "And how will we find my mother to deliver you?"

"We found you, didn't we?" I tell her. "We'll find your mother." I turn to Rosie. "And Wren. We'll find her, too."

"I know," she says to me, putting her arm around me. "We can do anything. Especially with your big brain."

We bump along in the back of the van and I feel an odd warm glow. She's right. We can do anything.

The road is getting rougher, so Louisa climbs back into her seat in the front, and Rosie and I brace ourselves along the side of the van, opposite Maddie and Jonah.

"We're going to need a plan," Maddie says, looking at me. She sounds like herself again, but the expression in her eyes is more intent, and more excited, than I remember. It's as though a spark that has been smoldering inside of her has just flamed to life.

"There might be something in the papers I have back at the car wash that can give us a clue about where to start looking for the Hornet," I say.

Rosie nods. "We'll have to plan on staying there a bit longer. If we go anywhere near any of our houses, we risk coming to the attention of the Alliance."

"No way," Maddie says, cradling the box in her palm. "Madeleine Frye, daughter of the Hornet, is not letting the Alliance get anywhere near this."

Louisa turns in the front seat to say, "And we're not letting them get anywhere near you."

"That sounds like something to discuss over lunch," Ryan announces over his shoulder. "I could really go for some soylami and a berry bar." He smiles at Rosie. "Radio ahead, Alpha team leader, and tell the others to prepare a banquet."

Rosie pulls the phone from her pocket and starts pushing buttons.

Maddie's eyes are wide. "What is that thing?" She frowns. "How do you have berry bars? And what is this car wash place?"

"We have a *lot* to tell you," Louisa says, and it's clear she's proud. "While you've been living the life at the

Phoenix Center, we've been running for ours. We even crossed the Settlement Lands. And you won't believe how Evelyn figured out where you were."

"I don't seem to be getting through," Rosie says, glaring at the phone. "We must be too far away."

"Keep trying," Ryan tells her. "I bet they're just busy gorging themselves on my lunch."

Louisa tells Maddie and Jonah about our journey as, next to me, Rosie repeats "Beta team, it's Alpha team, come in Beta team." I have the nagging feeling that there's a question I should be asking. Then I almost laugh when I realize there isn't, I feel that way just from force of habit. Although there's no denying that the force of that habit helped us find Maddie. And maybe it helped me find myself.

I think about how just two days ago my fingers were cramped from holding so tightly to my compass. But I'm starting to believe I can trust my own sense of direction. About all kinds of things.

My fingers go to the pocket of my sweatshirt and I reach inside and feel for the candy heart. I can't wait to tell Alonso about Phoenix Center. I picture his smile and the way he tilts his head to get his hair out of his eyes and I hear his voice saying, *Trust me*, and my heart does this funny little flipping thing.

I look around the van at Rosie next to me, and Maddie and Jonah talking quietly across from us, and Ryan and Louisa in front, and I can't help smiling. We did it. We got Maddie back. We're together again.

"Now arriving at home sweet home," Ryan announces like a tour guide. "Please keep your —"

He slams on the brakes, hard, sending us all banging into one another.

"What's wrong?" I ask, gripping the back of his seat to steady myself.

"It's gone," Ryan says.

"What do you mean it's go —"

But I don't finish my question because the answer is right in front of me. Where our headquarters were, there is now flat pavement crisscrossed with dusty tire tracks. A large pile of rubble off to one side is the only sign that anything ever stood here.

There is no car wash.

There is no sign of our camp.

There are no extra clothes, no sleeping bags, no water bottles, no clock, no supplies.

There is no trace of Helen, Drew, or Alonso.

What will happen tomorrow?
Read on for a preview of
Tomorrow Girls #4: Set Me Free.

Louisa, Jonah, and I set out early. The sky is streaked dull gray and pale yellow, and a ghostly wind howls.

We've left the others sleeping, both because they need the rest and because we couldn't bear to say good-bye. We head northwest toward my apartment building. In the crumbling townhouses that line the streets only a few windows are lit. I imagine sleepy employees getting ready for the early work shift or a world-weary insomniac sitting quietly in the early morning gloom, wondering what will become of all of us.

Jonah is no stranger to the streets at this hour, so I give him the address and we let him take the lead. I can tell Louisa is terrified, jumping at every sound. She hugs herself against the brutal slicing of the wind and stays close at my heels. It occurs to me how courageous of her it was to volunteer for this mission. And how incredibly loyal. How could I have ever doubted her?

We pass an alley, and I get the distinct feeling there are eyes staring out at us. I walk a little faster. The buildings cast deep, charcoal-toned shadows, which make everything much creepier.

"It's too dark," Louisa says, clearly sharing my thoughts. "Why don't we walk up on the El tracks? We'll have better visibility."

"And fewer dark alleys," Jonah adds.

I nod at them, feeling grateful that they've thought of this.

The El trains haven't run in years, not since the government decided it required too much energy to run them. The three of us carefully take the stairs to the elevated tracks. As we walk along the rusted rails, rats scuttle along at the far edges of the platform, and occasionally a filthy pigeon will swoop down so close I can actually see its beady little oil-slick eyes.

"At least we don't have to worry about a train coming at us," Louisa remarks.

The words are barely out of her mouth when I notice something approaching from the opposite direction, following the track at a steady, purposeful pace.

Heading right for us.

I squint into the growing daylight, hoping my eyes are playing tricks on me. But they aren't.

There is something moving toward us, all right. On a collision course.

It is definitely not a train.

But I almost wish it were.

POISON APPLE BOOKS

The Dead End

This Totally Bites!

Miss Fortune

Now You See Me...

Midnight Howl

Her Evil Twin

Curiosity Killed the Cat

At First Bite

THRILLING.
BONE-CHILLING.
THESE BOOKS
HAVE BITE!